I would like to dedicate my first book to the audience!

Author name Jayanth Kumar R

ISBN-13: 9798822012950

Publisher Kindle Direct Publishing

SON OF WOUNDED BUTTERFLY

Description

This story is a combination of presence and Intangible reality.
A fictional story of a mother and son with a lot of lives
who travel along in the journey, a village named flying hills,
which is specialized in farming the various breeds of
butterfly, once upon a time while the butterfly
hovering around in the garden a devil who comes
in seeking for the color from it and who achieved,
but this mystery travel lets you find
how did they live rest of their lives with
the only wing.

Art of Annihilation

Contents

WAVE OF A DELUSION

Beautiful notions that hailing into the wounds of portrayal, philosophies that rearing as lesions in the hands of illusionist, mysterious fog that summoned the mischiefs from the world of ruins, meanwhile the violent shadows were gliding towards the sky, until the creator waylaid from the cosmos having a fragmented wing with a colossal righteous, the one dedicated to tranquil the annihilated pessimistic, although chapters spinning as amusement, pacifying grin influx from the creator as a gust which revolt's into the freezing night formed by the spell of an illustration, innermost of it an aura climbing the upstairs intensely concerned for a pulsating flutter sound from a room, flutter amplifies also intensified to his sense as he gets closer, the boy looks at the door curiously then gradually opened the door and steps inside, as soon as the boy entered he could decipher rare pattern butterflies astonishing entire room wall, he steps in slowly observing at tiny butterflies flapping the wings at a snail's pace around every corner and he turns wondering at the arrival of a guest out of the blue, he bound where a white moonlight sailing from the broken window towards the long mirror inside the room, he wonders at the astonishing white ray and steps further towards mirror to see himself, all of a sudden tons of butterflies on the wall began to fly in full swing within the room, his eye reflects with magnificent colored butterflies spreading enormously, boy stood opposite to the rays of moonlight, butterflies on the wing above his head glowing from the beam of moonlight, some are fluttering on his shoulders and some orbiting in front of his eye, boy blushed looking at the pretty miniature's and tried touching it, the glow of happiness is profound in the atmosphere, likewise anonymous in his heart scattering from wings above the air, the boy striving to touch the butterflies in the air, by then he heard a preach which resembling to a blue whale from an immense depth of a sea, spinning butterflies remains stunned in the air and the boy unfocused from the tiny, smiles that faded into the deep seas, made the boy to slowly turn back and forth looking for the echo but the moonlight from the window is quietly turning off and on, he looks at tranquil butterflies floating in the air exchanging its hue from the rays of moon, he gets distracted from the fluctuation of moonlight and walks closer to the window, he noticed huge wings that is covering most of the sky light from outside the window, he could make out a shrouded enormous flapping echo emerging steadily from a long way towards him, while gazing at gigantic butterfly he could find a little glossing particle next to him passing across his cheeks from the corner side of window, boy's eye followed the floating particles and turns back to the interior of the room and saw the tiny butterflies inside the room floating in the air with no action but starts to emit the shining particles from its wings, boy looked intently at the sparkles that is slowly floating down, gradually he turns around and saw the entire room is entailing with the shining powder, as in when moonlight passing in and out from the window, particles are glooming back to back which brings a slight smile and he closes his eye and feels the particles floating towards his eye lashes, by the time particles reach his eye flicks, yet again he heard powerful voice of a huge butterfly and the reverberation of its wing, the giant has arrived closer to the window and acquired the whole moonlight from the sky, boy stood in the room filled with a shadows of giant, he quickly turned opening his eye to witness the diviner, but all of a sudden the atmosphere turned to morning and the boy relapsed into the natural world, the dusky night blended to the essence of titans sunrise, utter novelty evaporated like a mystic dice, swift variation in the ambiances diffused the eyes out of ordinary, in contrast to a clever carroty ray of light from the broken window sailing towards the sleeping eye, in most of it few glowing dust particles united with the rays and submerging to a strange cave, boy in the bed observing the flying dusts and gradually lifts his cute tiny hands, the moment his hand entered the rays consciousness dwelt identically with frosting aura, vibes reminiscent to an haulage of the giant hands from those deep seas rushing towards the exposure of warm sunlight out of the aquatic world, despite the fact that his hands in the bond of sun ray trying to connect with the blended dust particles, boy moves his hand sideways to get in contact with them nevertheless brilliant particles dodging from his association, he gets keen in touching them and they are unseen while catching in a frame, a flute harmony surf in room and the dust particles hovering in same rhythm, boy swops his eye towards roof and looked at the shadows of a tiny bird murmuring behind orange window, he kept staring at bird moving left to right and the shadow bird once again symphonies like a flute and up stretched steadily in a place lifting its wings for some time, in few seconds another bird from a long distance responded echoing in a similar symphony, sudden step sound in the stairs made bird at roof to fly away, laying boy gets distracted and got up with his blanket, looking at the door consciously, sound of a climbing steps gradually increases and the boy crawls towards edge of the bed gazing at the door confusingly for a strange activity, but however stair climbing party reached, though the person about to open the boy's room door by then

"Yamuna come here!!" shouts a base voiced character,

party outside the door steps down after receiving the command from downstairs, the boy relaxed a little for nobody entering his room, he got down from his bed and slowly looking at the enigmatic space suspiciously, next to his bed he found a desk loaded with lot of books, color sheets and paint boxes which is unorganized, he walks towards the table and something shove his feet, he looks down it's a mixed colored paintbrush lying down, he glanced for a while and picks it up, slowly carries to the desk and retained upon it, meantime he saw few books on the table and some sheets were stuffed with a fascinating paint of a sunrise behind the lime hills and another few sheets are drawn with alphabet's in unique style, boy constantly stare's at the drawn paints, while the boy kept busy turning the paint book, within few moment a sin in the form of head pain acquired his mind severely, he holds his head and express his scream with a low voice and dwindle his face, boy walks back to the bed at slow pace and sat, he retained his hand on head and worrying about the excessive pain from his head, boy senses were similar to a suffocating fish abandoned out of the aqua world, while the pain increased in his head, boy closes his eye and a pitch dark vision made him to remind more of the sins in his mind but only in a form of ache, few second later the dark world had a flashing particles falling down like a snow, he feels little strange and unable to connect with the catastrophe but looks marvelous, pain from his head fades lower by little, and he turns out to be normal as a fish casting back to its ecology likewise a relaxation after the departure of sin is a way to rebirth in seventh heaven, the boy feels physical existence in the flow of pulse, he tries looking at his own hands and legs wondering

"Who am I?"

He turns around to explore the paranormal room and sounds out

"Where am I?"

The boy is not able to recall any of his past, but he could recall the butterflies in the room which has been restored by the dust particles, the moonlight rolled out with an orange light hitting from the regular window towards the very same mirror, Bhadra walks towards the orange rays, his eye occupied with a lot of brightness and obviously, his body temperature slightly up, Bhadra tries to turn back towards the mirror by the time he turns around to scout his appearance, party from the downstairs started to climb the stairs all over again, Bhadra frightened, his heart started to beat rapidly, also tries to step back towards his bed slowly looking at the door and hearing to the extensive footstep, as the step increased the boy got scared and started crying very loud looking at the door in addition of wiping his tears, but the unstoppable time drifted and set to open the door,

A mysterious enchantress at the door whispered,

"Good morning my dear",

The boy tried lifting his head to recognize the party's face but he couldn't tilt up, somewhat obstructing his neck to see a godlike being, Bhadra in wet eyes holding his neck and again tries tilting up, a person near the door began to walk closer to him. The boy feels a positive vibration while Yamuna walks closer to him,

"Who made you cry my lovely doll, don't worry I am here for you now, I won't leave you alone again okay? Stop crying now and come to me, my angel",

He stood steadily at the position without moving, the moment when Yamuna came closer to Bhadra it seemed fairly true to its life of the hands presence to uplift, Bhadra into her trustful arms, while the lift feels alike enchanted force coasting towards his desire and a gravitational force inviting the star to its universe, Bhadra sitting on her left hand side and able to notice her from one side, by then his tears turned to solid alike the separate soil at the shattering desert, Bhadra kept envisioning the similar shining particles on her cheek, Yamuna walks carrying him and Bhadra feels the rhythm that floats on top of a sea wave, her kiss on his cheeks connects the sea with replicating lavish sky, the room seems unsolved puzzle after Bhadra viewing from her arms, Yamuna sets him down to bath and Bhadra again unable to lift his head to see her, but she started pouring hot water upon him, Bhadra looks at those invisible shiny water passing through his eyes and mist around him is flying and disappearing in seconds, the boy turned towards Yamuna and his inner voice trying to ask her,

"Who am I? Why is it that I can't lift my head to see you? Who are you exactly to me?"

His vocal trapped in the deep seas and enslaved on flying at external bio network, unspoken inner self was a discontinued legacy. She tried dressing Bhadra in various clothes, but although none of them appeared to be good on him, she messes up the entire wardrobe searching for a good one, hardly a few minutes of scrambling the wardrobe seems worth mixing to pick up a new T-shirt in a plastic pack, she takes out the T-shirt from the plastic cover, the orange-colored dashing T-shirt glows him up, she reads out the wording tattooed on it, which says an apple a day keeps anyone away if you throw it hard enough, Yamuna reads the slogan and laughs loud,

"Can't you shower him later, you fool I am late for the office already," says father,

The uncontrollable base voice from downstairs made Yamuna panic and run toward Krishna,

"Bhadra, you sit here and I will be back with the breakfast and tablets for you," says mother Yamuna,

"Look at the way you have packed my lunch box! You have loaded the whole ration in it! How am I supposed to take it to the office?" asked Krishna,

"I will fix it in a few seconds," says Yamuna,

She picks up the lunch box and ran inside the kitchen to settle it,

"Are you bringing it or shall I leave to the office?" says Krishna,

Yamuna gets back the Lunch box after fixing it, while Bhadra again walks toward the mirror to see himself, by then a dense sound of steel boxes hitting the wall and spinning in the air, a continuous slap kind of noise echoes till Bhadra's room at the upstairs, Yamuna returned to Bhadra’s room with breakfast and Bhadra's with his wedged neck looking at her feet and saw tears dropping down from Yamuna, Bhadra tries to lift his head holding his neck but the circumstances were unfortunate, Yamuna came closer to Bhadra and picks him up and made him sit upon his bed and fed him, she picks up a small piece of bread and Bhadra looking her hands coming closer to him, the boy feeling strange, she made him open his mouth and fed him, the boy had the bread in his mouth and started to chew, the moment he crushes the toasted bread in his mouth he feels an astonishing seawater with candy in a shape of a wave passing in front. Bhadra enjoys the bread mixed with vegetables, his hunger gets loaded with energy and auras of relaxation,

“By the time I manage all other work, I am unable to concentrate on you!” says concerned Yamuna,

Bhadra could sense the power of life esteemed in her voice, but he feels much safer to be with her, and the cells of confidence within him are strengthening like an Ozone layer concealing the planet.

A primary school student whose few days of concern for being a watercolorist and he is very keen on finding a real-time illustration to capture in his visual sensation and to succeed in an upcoming painting contest at his school, unfortunately, any frame he overcame, there was a wing combined to the captures which lead the frames flying away from his cognizance, some other ideas fitting in his frame were already tamed by the first part of souls, the boy in search of a good idea’s that are left in the blue water and the best one is passing in a magical train at blue mere, his survival predestined to a lost cruise, and he is known as Tapi. He always desired to be successful in the contest alike every year and also his parents wanted him to accomplish it, however, the realness from Tapi himself was because he collapsed in the sphere of unfolding an art thing in his nature but the endurance kept him pushing further trying to something very unique in every year contest, though his art seems like unsurprising, he is still a price winning artist at the school for every year and somewhere close to the best one, he always won second prize in drawing category and participants the participants were only two members! Yes, he is winning the second prize while there are only two participants in it, like every day, Tapi and his close friend Saagar are now walking together to school.

"Do you know any bookstore nearby?" asks Tapi,

"For what?" Saagar asked,

"I need to buy a painting box for today's competition"

"I think there is one stall behind this road, come will take you there," says Saagar,

"Why are you so serious about this contest? Are there any prizes for winners?" asks Saagar,

"Yes, there are some awards distributed this year," replied Tapi,

While the boys talking to each other arrived at bookstore road,

"Can you see that? The shop is right over there," said Saagar, and pointed to a small shop,

"Saagar! This road has an only shop, everyone can see that dude!" says Tapi,

Boys went to the book store

"Need a paint box," says Tapi,

Shopkeeper brought few collection then arranged them on table, collections are quite interesting and Tapi gets engaged in selecting them, besides Saagar checks out unique inventions inside the store, every object displayed in the store possessing him to buy however some desires in this world are fulfilled by currency only, his vision floating on every color and it stopped when he got to see a watermelon kind of object within the glass stand, Saagar looking at the unique eraser and wondering it's roseate color, his observation seems like if there are any opportunity for him to hold it, he wouldn't hesitate putting them in his mouth if any, Saagar slaps his ties checking his pockets for some money but was left only with unfortunate, gradually his vision sailed towards another key bunch seemed yellow tinted dashing mango fruit, his glorious receiver accepting the maximum love on the object, he kept watching the desirable makes, finish of each and every product in the store that looks so amazingly real like a freshly chopped fruits, his eye seems unmovable, his desires are unbreakable, his hands were also uncontrollable as they try gliding towards the desire to communicate with fruits by then the owner caught him by knocking his head and questioned,

"Do you want to buy them?" asked Shopkeeper,

Saagar looked at the shopkeeper helplessly,

"Which one shall I choose?" asks Tapi interrupting the situation,

Tapi broke their minus wave, Saagar confusingly looked at Tapi,

"I am confused with a lot many good options over here buddy, can you help me to select the best one?" asks Tapi,

Saagar had a style,

"Now we have a confusing situation here, it's a very difficult thing to say... which is the masterpiece over here?" says Saagar and kept thinking,

He acts like an expert watercolorist, who chooses his painting things very carefully but actually, he is not!

“Nothing fools, both do the same art, they are just made with different boxes,” says shopkeeper,

Interrupted Saagar from his expert review, seems defenseless and he found one of the paint boxes with a fruit design in the front panel of it and Saagar thinks the box should be a good option to buy only because it had a fruit embossed on it and with a confident smile he lifts his head towards the shopkeeper, but the shopkeeper is already staring at him sarcastically, Saagar feels awkward and turns back to Tapi,

“I feel this fruit designed box does great paintings!” says Saagar,

Tapi is speechless.... staring at Saagar and turns doubtfully turned back to the shopkeeper and told,

“I will buy this one,” says Tapi and selects the paintbox suggested by Saagar,

The shopkeeper grabs money from Tapi's hands and pushes the selected pain box onto the table, Tapi lifts the paintbox lying on the table and he slightly opened them and he could gradually feel the enormous glow popping out from within the paint box, the amazing color chalks and a cute paintbrush on the left-hand side, happiness and most important confidence that is slightly boosting Tapi’s mood, Saagar looking at the colors which are reminding him the Choco fruits with different colors that he kept buying in the store,

“This paint color blocks seem like chocolate that he had in the bottle,” says Saagar and kept looking at the paintbox,

“Enough of watching, let's go we are already late,” says Tapi,

He closes the paintbox delicately and places them inside his bag gradually zipping them back from the other end, while a lady voice calling out his name resonates in the wind, Tapi turns back and he saw his aunt Yamuna, happily and also surprisingly looking at him, Yamuna holding the vegetable basket in her hands and slowly walked towards Tapi.

“What are you doing here?” asks Yamuna with a smile,

“We have a painting competition today in school, so came to buy the paint boxes,” says Tapi,

“Extraordinary, come let's have breakfast,” asks Yamuna,

“No I have to leave,” says Tapi with an embarrassed smile reaction,

“It's ok come,” says Yamuna,

She holds Tapi's hands and forcefully took him to the house, Saagar feels strange,

“You too are my son dear, walk with me,” says Yamuna,

Yamuna walks crossing the road with Tapi’s hands and Tapi holds Saagar's hands and dragged him together, meantime while Tapi and Saagar climbs the stair to Yamuna’s house,

“How is your mom Tapi?” asks aunt Yamuna,

“Nice aunt, she might visit you in the evening,” says Tapi entering inside,

“Good, I heard your mom....”

Yamuna's words were missed by Tapi he got diverted completely towards a strange small dude sitting on a chair, away from the entrance of the house, Tapi curiously looked at the stranger,

"He is your cousin," says Yamuna to Tapi,

"Oh" smiles Tapi looking at Yamuna,

"You guys keep talking to him, I will come back with the breakfast for you," says Yamuna,

Bhadra bent his head looking at his feet and swinging them, Tapi slowly went closer to him.

"Hey, hi," says Tapi,

"Don't worry? I'm your cousin" says Tapi,

Bhadra is looking at Tapi without any eye blink, and Yamuna came with the breakfast,

"First have the breakfast, here you go," says Yamuna,

Gave them plates and a glass of water, Saagar's eyes were flourishing looking at the colorful vegetables in the breakfast and he rapidly starts over to eat, Tapi looked at his cousin and gradually consumes with a curious feeling about his cousin who seemed strange, Yamuna comes back,

"How is the breakfast my dear," asks Yamuna,

"Awesome!" shouts excited Saagar,

"Shall I get you some more?" asks Yamuna,

“No, we already had in our houses while leaving!” says Tapi,

Yamuna took the plates and water glasses once they finished,

Tapi and Saagar after finishing the breakfast got up from their chairs and walked closer to Bhadra, Tapi gets emotionally happy with the feeling of having a brother, Tapi experience his surround in slow motion for a while walking towards Bhadra,

“Our hearts were unwilling to listen to the loneliness of a nature, which lead winds to sail invisible and the waters to flow unseen yet to be lived by creators of the bond when the wishes for one were always satisfied by the nature of time.”

While these words were streaming as a feeling in his heart, he walked toward him speechless, and Saagar knocked Bhadra’s head strongly, Bhadra throws back with a strong look to Saagar,

“Hey, why are you hurting my cousin,” says Tapi and grabs Saagar’s hand,

“Dude, I just got scared, he is staring back like a killer,” says Saagar,

Saagar gets closer to his face,

“My God! His eye seems very dangerous!” told Saagar,

Tapi grabs Saagar’s hair and pulls back his head holding them, by then Yamuna walks with a glass of milk,

“Bhadra, this is your cousin... say hi to him!” told Yamuna,

Bhadra just looked at Tapi and Saagar without speaking,

“Aunt, he is already old enough right, when will he start talking to?” asks Tapi,

“Very soon Tapi,” said Yamuna,

“My mother once told, even I started to speak after few months, and she complained that I became a big headache for them,” says Tapi,

“Aw! Nothing much, you were a beautiful kid even then” reacts Yamuna,

“Then, how come she said, I use to speak all day by asking a lot of questions to everyone?” asks Tapi,

“Asking questions is a sign of a good child dear don’t worry, she doesn’t have the patience to clear your doubts kid,” says Yamuna,

“I believe even Bhadra will start talking too much once he begins to speak, Later he might start coming with us to the school right aunt?” asks Tapi,

“Yes, by now he should have been in your school but your principal is not letting him,” says Yamuna,

“Why aunt? What happened?” asks Tapi,

“She was a little bit strict when I met her, she spoke to my son and Bhadra failed to respond her back, then she says, he will be given admission to the school only when he learns to speak and she wants him to be very smart at least verbally, even we are trying our best to prepare him as per the requirement,” says Yamuna,

“Aunt there are many children in the school who are not that good at speaking,” says Tapi,

"Yes, my husband always said that it is the responsibility of an institution to make him speak well and prepare him for his future, that should be the purpose of a school," said Yamuna,

"Uncle beats him?" asks Tapi,

"His father cares for him too much, he tries conversing with him but Bhadra is not reacting neither comes out of the silence, we do not know what is the right way for him to start responding," says Yamuna,

"Aunt, did you take him to the hospital?" asks Tapi,

"We have already consulted doctors Tapi, they told us to communicate with him frequently from day and night and if not, the last option would be the operation but by then he should be able to talk very soon now we have trained him few speeches already, he just learned very few responses, by next year he will be in the schools Tapi," says Yamuna,

"Hoping soon aunt," says Tapi,

"Your mother suggested me take him to the temple near your house Tapi,

"Yes, my mother said it is an amazing place aunt, god in there has a lot of power he will give anything if we seek him by praying honestly, I think even we should take Bhadra over there, he will bless Bhadra also, then he will be able to communicate with us right?" asks Tapi,

"Yes, we are consulting doctors and we are seeking god's blessing also, that is why we are confident that he will be able to communicate with us very soon, hence I told you from next year he is going to join you for the school and you are the one has to take him daily along with you to the school for few years, okay?" asks Yamuna,

"Aunt does he know to pronounce alphabets?" asks Tapi,

"He just started to pronounce a few words Tapi, but he does amazing paints, and he sometimes does speak while drawing, but after that, he will not open his mouth only!" says Yamuna,

"Wow is he interested in drawings? That sounds great! Then we have a new painter for our school from next year" says Tapi,

"I think you should check out his drawings, wait I will bring his book, you will be amazed looking at it," says Yamuna running towards the upstairs,

Tapi and Saagar looked at Bhadra bent his heads down and merged his two hands finger together and forming them like a bird and waving them like a bird flapping in the clouds,

"Dude this is your hand, not a bird that can fly high!" said Saagar,

"Keep quiet let's watch him," says Tapi,

Yamuna got down the stairs with a notebook in her hand and opens them while walking toward the boys, the very first page consists of a painting of stone sculpted with a blue sky where the clouds are full of fire and the burning birds that are falling to the rivers, the amazing paint radiating into the boy's eye.

"Wow, wonderful!" says Tapi,

"Yeah, it is amazing Aunt," says Saagar,

Tapi received the book from Yamuna, and he turns the page, got to see a boy inside the room along with a lot of butterflies flying around him and a boy jumping to catch those shining sparkles dropping from the flutter of butterflies above him, Tapi looking at it and left speechless at the glowing page.

"Aunt this is an amazing drawing, I have never seen anything such in real nor an illustration, I can't believe that our Bhadra has such a brilliant visual talent in him," says Tapi,

"Check a few more pages Tapi, still a lot more to go," says Yamuna,

Tapi smiles looking at Yamuna and Bhadra,

"Give me some idea?" asks Tapi to Bhadra,

Unvoiced Bhadra looks bizarre, Saagar turned pages looking at many artworks done only by Bhadra,

"All of this done only by Bhadra?" asks Saagar,

"Yes, all alone by Bhadra," says Yamuna,

"My God, Amazing...... So many..." says Saagar and turns the pages faster,

"Hey, wait!" says Tapi to Saagar and stops at a page,

Art of two schoolboys with a wall clock in their hands and talking to a butterfly and a boy aside,

"This is nothing, let me show you another amazing wait," says Saagar and turns the page backward faster and stops,

A giant flying creature pumps the waters from its mouth along with a few small flies around it.

“Wow! This is seriously amazing...” says Tapi,

Speechless Tapi... for a second wondering at the pain,

“Aunt can you please permit me to take this book along with me?” asks Tapi,

“Take it, you don’t need a permit for that!” responded Yamuna,

“I will return this by sunset since I need this as a reference for my drawing competition!” says Tapi,

“Sure Tapi! Please take it,” says Yamuna,

Tapi took Bhadra’s painting book and puts it in the bag,

“Aunt are you coming to the school event today with my mom?” asks Tapi,

“I haven't communicated with your mother yet Tapi, if possible, I might come,” said Yamuna,

“Please join us without miss aunt, because I am participating today and I will get the price,” says Tapi,

“You are confident and that’s great dear it’s like you have already won, I will come!” says Yamuna,

“What are you participating at dear,” asks Yamuna to Saagar,

“I am doing a skit with my classmates” lies Saagar and looks at Tapi,

“Okay aunt, we are getting late for the school, we have to leave,” says Tapi,

“Ok bye dear, and all the best for your competition!” says Yamuna,

Tapi and Saagar walked out of the door and waved hands to Yamuna and Bhadra, Tapi looks at Bhadra while stepping down the stairs and he is staring at Tapi and his bag, Tapi turns around and with a smile and walks out of the gate,

Yamuna closes the door and lifts Bhadra and sings a song,

The god inside us was always murmuring, like a sun and moon...
The smile inside us was always motivating, like a mind in the wind...
...
...

Suddenly the doorbell rang! Yamuna stops singing and drops Bhadra at the chair and turns back to the door a few seconds later she walks to the door and opens it, it was Tapi and Saagar again!

“Did you forget anything boys?” asks Yamuna,

“Aunt, can I take Bhadra with me just for seeing around,” asks Tapi,

Yamuna with the suffocated smile did not respond,

“Anyway, today there will be no one in the school to ask us because everybody is occupied with preparation for the annual event happening in the evening,” says Saagar,

Yamuna thinking...

"It will be an advantage for Bhadra to come out of the house and join our friends to communicate which helps him to get improved," says Tapi,

"Since he has never seen the school right and it's completely our responsibility to take care of him without a glitch!" says Saagar,

"He can make some new friends at the school and there are many people who get connected well with Bhadra," says Tapi,

"Yeah, but I have never left him alone Tapi, I'm a little worried about him!" says Yamuna,

"However, you will join us in the evening at the school event right, then you can take him back with you," says Tapi,

"Yes, but I'm not afraid of that point Tapi!" says Yamuna,

"Bhadra will surely admire the annual function that is happening in the evening, please send him with us aunt, I will make him talk with others and take care of him safely," said Saagar,

"Dear, he has medication to take! He should have them on time, so next time you can take him" confronts Yamuna,

"Give his tablets to us aunt, we will make sure he has them on time!" says Saagar,

"I have cough tablets to consume in the afternoon, at that time I will feed him his medicines!" says Tapi,

Yamuna thinks again for a while, she turns back to Bhadra inside the house sitting alone on a chair, and turns back to Tapi, thinks for a while...

"Okay but you shouldn't leave him alone, you have to keep him with you where ever you go, you should take him with you anywhere you go along with his tablets and lunch that's your responsibility, will you?" asks Yamuna,

"Sure aunt!" says Tapi,

Tapi and Saagar smiled at each other, Yamuna walked inside and picks up Bhadra from the chair and sets him down near the door, Tapi tries to hold his hands and Bhadra failed to respond to him then Saagar takes the chance, raising his hand to him and Bhadra lifts his hand towards the Saagar, which made Yamuna and Tapi astound at his response towards Saagar!

"Not bad Saagar, very good..." says Yamuna with a smile,

"Just a moment... wait here," said Yamuna and went inside,

Yamuna returns with a small cover, she loads them into Tapi's bag,

"Here you go, it has a bread jam, he likes the most and Tablets which he doesn't like the most, and you guys should make him have without a miss," says Yamuna,

"Sure... aunt I will!" says Tapi,

She loads the cover into the bag,

"I had no plans to attend the event, but now I have to right! At least I need to come for picking him up" says Yamuna with a little worried expression,

“Aunt by the time you arrive, we will prepare him well and you will be surprised looking at his responses, and I make sure of it,” says Saagar and

As the sparkles in the sky, three of them kept moving,

FLUTTER OF CHRONICLES

Unspoken caterpillars sailing in the woods that may inferno, entire branches dissolved but the destiny cloaked inside the memo, phases of emotions in the edge always wanted to fly solo, from the beautiful wings to form united there was a mile of a journey towards hallow. Bhadra connected with Saagar simultaneously paced out of the house holding his hands, while a blessing of conscious that insists the space in rotating towards a spectating helpful ray stood near portal smiling at him with tears in her eye besides an alternative down on one's luck about tilting his perception to see his mother nevertheless bound to a spell disabled him to witness the graces of divine, yet an absence of storming tears neither an agony pacing in the fear since the wings were always meant to fly in one dimension at a peer.

"Dude, what's the plan after the participation?" asks Saagar,

"Enjoying the event with the audience, right?" asks Tapi,

"Instead, you join us for a different thing this time," told Saagar,

"Join, for what?" asks Tapi,

"Dude, don't you know? We are activating last year's plan..." says Saagar,

Confused look from Tapi,

"Visiting flying hills buddy!" said Saagar,

"Isn't it prohibited to go without a teacher's permission?" asks Tapi,

“We have the best planning buddy, trust me!” replied Saagar,

“Do you know the consequences, what if the principal gets to know about it, I feel you guys are going to face a big issue!” said Tapi,

“Buddy... let me tell you something, last year there were nine different batches found by our seniors in the flying hills, all of them were from our school, did anyone know about it?” said Saagar,

Tapi in a shock,

“Yes, many of them skipped our school event and had a blast in the flying hills man!” said Saagar,

“If everyone is going, it doesn’t mean we should also break the rule Saagar, we still do have a lot many things to do in our school event,” said Tapi,

“It’s completely a boring thing to be at the school event, we don’t have anything new buddy, it's the same as every year,” said Saagar,

“Aren’t you aware of the scary house this year?” asks Tapi,

The unenthusiastic look of Saagar,

“Our seniors have worked hard constantly for a few months to create the best scary house for this event, it’s a very new thing in our entire town and this isn’t tried out by any of the schools, it will be amazing for sure!” says Tapi,

Wondering Saagar,

“Last week some of our classmates had been to that scary house while the seniors were still preparing, and some of them are speechless about its recreation dude, I suggest you guys don't miss it!" said Tapi,

The sarcastic look of Saagar was unexpected, while Tapi is still missing them in the event,

"At least can you wait for me until I get the reward? So that, even I can try joining you" asks Tapi,

But Saagar holding Bhadra's hands kept walking without any response and Bhadra isn't anxious about their conversation and was occupied with the tone of the public atmosphere,

"Dude, none of us wants to miss our plan this year, especially mentioning to watching some nonsense scary houses is of no use, no matter what! We will not be there at school for even a single minute when the show starts! Although we are planning to leave the school early or at the time when the event begins and I am hundred percent sure that no one will notice us moving out because we do have plan B" says Saagar,

"What? No, it's not a waste of time, our seniors have planned it precisely" said Tapi,

"Every year the seniors kept tossing the same thing again and again, they always failed to create something new and it's the same crap of outcome that repeats, we don't want to take a chance of sitting and keep clapping the whole day at a dispirited show, going to the hills is next level of experience and the fun that you are going to miss buddy!" said Saagar,

"I am unable to understand your takes man," said Tapi,

"Wait for the show to end, you will understand the real thing to experience of being in the hills!" replied Saagar,

Tapi smiles sarcastically looking at Saagar,

"If you had known the history of flying hills, by this time you would have joined our batch and shouldn't have this smile on your face dude!" replied Saagar,

Bhadra is looking at Saagar's excited reaction,

"What do you think, do I come from out of space every day?" asks Tapi,

"Why do you think the scary house is better than flying hills? It's because you haven't heard about the experience of being there" replied Saagar,

"Even I have heard the stories from our families, but nobody has seen that giant right, I know man" replied Tapi,

"It's not that easy to achieve a historical giant but one or the other day we will!" said Saagar,

Tapi suddenly turned towards Saagar, and started to laugh a loud looking at him,

"First of all, do you have the strength in you to climb the hill?" asked Tapi,

"We will fly easily," said Saagar,

Tapi smiled looking at Saagar,

"Did you know, once our classmates went there and they were unable to reach the top on time due to some people in the team were incapable of and by that time they began to return then it was late in the evening and they got stuck at a dark puzzle up there, I suggest you people don't just attempt blindly without knowing! Saagar, it is easy to decide and being another stupid from our school" says Tapi,

"The last one was nice," says Saagar looking at Tapi,

"Tapi, my mother always told me it is a place where gods exist, and the places like that cannot have negativity in it, I agree it is hard to climb and I am also confident our team is strong buddy, from past one week we all are into exercises!" said Saagar,

"Yeah, now I wonder why you guys were running in the ground even after the school hours" addressed Tapi,

"The gang who were stuck in the hills... None of them knew a proper route for the hilltop, hence they were confused and trapped in the middle of the forest, but I know the perfect route for the hilltop, so not to worry," says Saagar,

"But you keep yourself updated that there are a lot of many animals that come out of the forest to roads in the evening and you guys are going in the evening at the time of event begins, What you do then?" asks Tapi,

"Dude you are less aware of the hill, can you stop trying to divert us?" said Saagar,

"You are just misguiding us and want us to be scared because you too are..." said Saagar,

"Your mythical words don't work here Tapi, leave I will take Cheyyar with me up there and come back safely," said Saagar,

"I am not trying to misguide you!" says Tapi,

"And I not less aware of the hill?" asks Tapi,

"You are!" said Saagar,

"Do you know what the name of the region called is?" asks Tapi,

"Flying hills!" said Saagar,

"Do you know how the name was retained?" asks Tapi,

Tapi showering questions to Saagar,

"Oh, you are just trying to ask something else now," said Saagar,

Sarcastically smiled Tapi,

"Listen to me now," said Tapi,

Saagar turned towards Tapi, Bhadra too,

"The only hill station in the world that consists of a large number of butterflies population is our flying hills! Therefore, it's named after the specialty of our region" says Tapi,

"Yes, everybody knows that dude!" smiled Saagar,

"Wait, I haven't completed yet," said Tapi,

Meanwhile, Bhadra was walking slowly and Saagar drags him with a hard pull,

"Walk a little faster dude," said Saagar,

Tapi hits Saagar from his hands to Saagar's shoulder for the unwanted act,

"Don't hurt my cousin" says Tapi,

"Ok, I'm sorry dear," asked Saagar to Bhadra smiling at him,

"It's ok listen, our lives and emotions are connected with the butterflies," says Tapi,

"Oh yeah, that stone in the hilltop, found by our ancestors, I have heard that too," asked Saagar,

"Dude! Wait until I complete, do not interrupt, listen to me completely" shouts Tapi,

"Cool buddy, don't get exhausted, please continue Tapi," said Saagar,

"While a tiny spark ignited between the sky and earth as a sunrise, a farmer walks in the misty hilltop in search of fire woods for the spark that lights his roof and grounds of few shelters, bundle of woods on his head made the man wiser from the years but the patterns that never stressed while they walked in the grasses of hills which pulled through a set of generations into the fortune, yet his progression was ongoing by then, his vision twirled towards a glowing white stone crowded with lot of butterflies upon it, wondering farmer kept the bundle aside and slowly walks towards it wondering on the glow, a slower step raised like a never stood sun, Farmer rushes towards the stone in a medium pace and the genius butterfly's flapped away and the stone started to emit a white flash immediately, Farmer covered his eye for the unstable beam and steps back, few minutes later he gradually took his hands back, an amazing white stone excites farmer to get closer, the beautiful sculpt and an impossible work on it makes it unique but the farmer did not understand anything of it, farmer whose fortune was only on the woods that make him and his clusters to be feasible to their destinies that gets composed, hours later he realized that the stone is no use for him apart from viewing, farmer walks back on the same grasses that showed him the wood and also forthcoming fondness to the spirits of public, farmer left the hills with some woods and lot of memories of an unusual flies and its shelter, farmer lifts the bunch of woods on his head and began to return singing a song,

Breezing fogs that follow, flying sunshine that shallow, inside the world of lovable ones...
Moon shards we barrow, homes light up with sorrow, gifted by a chosen of heavens...

Suddenly the farmer ends up singing a few words after looking at someone climbing the hills, without losing concentration farmer slowly walks down carefully holding the woods upon him firmly,

"For the woods huh," asks a farmer

"Have you left any for us?" asks anonymous

"The whole hill is for you, with a glowing stone on the top, enjoy them," said farmer,

Anonymous walker felt strange but kept moving upward, and the woods farmer carried were burnt as lighting in the world when the sun left asleep but darkness still lived till a feet distance to every mini lamp left in the houses, at late night the farmer completes his dinner and comes out of the house to wash his hand and saw the flying hills, a small spark shining at the tip but covered with little fog and the moon behind glowing happily, the farmer glances and went back to sleep, early morning next day the farmer again went to collect some woods and saw the huge crowd climbing the hills and once he reached the top, farmer rotated his head looked at the public arrived from the entire village to the hilltop kept pushing each other in front of the glowing stone to sight the unusual situation, however few villagers were scared of the tempo, few assumed it could be a God visit and few yet to figure the situation deeply but everybody had a confusion hence no one spoke, people were a silent spectator and then my grandfather who is actually the farmer all this time I kept talking about, he was the one to make out speak and also lead everyone to the conclusion," said Tapi,

"Oh, the farmer is your grandfather?" asks Saagar,

"Yes," said Tapi,

"What happened next?" asks Saagar,

"My grandfather told everyone that, let us name this stone as the blessing stone and leave it in the same spot as a showpiece to the visitors from the outside to come around our village, as the visitor gets increased, spontaneously our place will evolve as a tourist spot, however, our village is more attractive obviously and the unique stone makes an added advantage for us,

Villagers were confused by my grandfather's idea,

Grandfather looked at everyone and they all seem confused,

"Folks, the stone has a purpose to be here! We do not know for what, but the stone is one of us now, so I feel we can grow with this blessing, and make this a tourist place which will help our village in the economy and every individual can begin with your own business of your wish, let our children go to the schools, and we all need a good hospital right? How about good transportation? How about a developed town? and all these are possible from our ideas, our place already has a lot of history and we have beautiful visuals for side-viewing but the facility is not available for the tourist here, but which can be developed time by time, once everyone began generating money which should not be a worrying task but future of this town happens when the demand for this place increases right!

And the words from my grandfather seemed sensible to every villagers and they all came together agreeing to the idea, some of the villagers were busy understanding the written messages on glowing stone, some weren't bothered by what our ancestors wanted to pass on, because many families had completely lost hope in the giant, for some it was just a big joke or a diversion of the lifecycle, they didn't wanted to understand what could appear, they least believed that everybody's problem-solving formula could have been a imagination but never the reality, while a few people from the village still believed their history, they always had a hope to achieve to perceive the giant in their existence, but the stone had to see from an old man to a small cute girl staring at it, alike visiting a paint for a few hours, and some tried to decode the hint partially and some got confused and tried to create the history of their own in the process of assumptions, and some were passing time in front of the stone but what it says left a big mystery till now!" says Tapi,

"So, because of your grandfather, we are now going to school, your grandfather rocks Tapi," said Saagar,

"For many years topic of the town remained the same about the giant butterfly, which appears to save our lives! justify the struggle, overcome failures, the darkness which should turn into light and the change of generation, but few people from the town always laughed at our beliefs and history, it was always hard for them to accept or to convince a mentally ill right, but in our family; we always believed in it because my grandmother told us that once in a century there is chosen one born in our village to unleash the giant butterfly, and will be trained one to save our crowd from the attack of evil which drowns us to the darkness, and few of our people started feeling themselves as the chosen, and some hunted for the one, which went a big task for many of them but how they got to know wasn't a mystery it's the stone that divulges clearly,

Set

To release

Giant butterfly from his existence

Can never be elected but to take place

When a calm gust of uninvited negativity

Inward bound enchanting towards many lives

Awakens the giant to produce a huge blow

Of airstream with magnificent sparkles

In the direction of the special

To amend whole mobs

Destiny

Everyone is halfway decoding to understand what our lineages have sculpted for us, many people from this town want to overcome the darkness in their houses dominated by greediness, fakeness, hatred, and many more, every individual had an issue with at least any of these attached to us, a pure chosen one who would amend our fate was the history sayings and our family taught us to keep an eye on anonymous-looking, speaking and thinking people to doubt their destiny. But till now we haven't seen any of them alike buddy, this is how the history rolled in from our ancestors to us" says Tapi,

Bhadra imagines the enticing story illustrated by Tapi,

"Did you get it? The history never told, about a negative effect upon traveling to flying hills" said Saagar,

“As I already mentioned, it is a very easy decision to be another stupid from our school, history had never mentioned the risk but what about the future?” asks Tapi,

“I understand your concern buddy, but till now there has been nothing that happened and will not happen in the future too, you enjoy your scary house and other clapping sessions in the school. Myself, Cheyyar, and Bhadra will visit the flying hills to enjoy the view and return at the same time while the event ends in school” said Saagar,

“What, when did Bhadra join you? No way, this is not happening” said Tapi,

“Don’t worry, I will take care of him” says Saagar,

“You will take care of him? Buddy, you guys return safely first from flying hills” says Tapi,

“We will! don’t worry, Bhadra trust’s me a lot more than you, so I believe he will be happy to join us” said Saagar,

Saagar looks at Bhadra and then asks,

“Bhadra, are you ready to go with us?” asks Saagar,

Bhadra walks looking at the public, some of them are waving hands at Bhadra wishing him a smile and he is not able to concentrate on Saagar and Tapi’s conversations.

“I am not letting you take Bhadra for the hills Saagar, don’t even dare, it’s a big risk, I am responsible to take care of him, or else my aunt will scold me,” said Tapi,

“Don't worry Tapi, I'm there right, even I have to come safely and we will” said Saagar,

“I know very well about you Saagar... you guys are very irresponsible, you people enjoy there at hills, myself and Bhadra will go to the scary house and later we will watch the show,” said Tapi,

“If you leave Bhadra with us it would be an advantage for him Tapi, we will not force him to speak but when the journey begins, he will be observing our conversations and it would organically allow him to respond and nevertheless the journey will be a fascinated one for him since he might have not seen anything apart from his house,” said Saagar,

“Specially mentioning that I don’t want Bhadra with you guys at any crisis, you and Cheyyar is specialized in teaching most unnecessary things, and irresponsible too, so I don’t want to commit any kind of risk, instead I have a better plan, I will leave Bhadra with Hemavati she is our class representative with a very good communication skill and Bhadra will be with us in the rehearsals, that would engage him,” says Tapi,

Tapi looks at Bhadra,

“Don’t worry I have better plans for you,” says Tapi,

Bhadra stops walking suddenly and admires looking at something, Tapi and Saagar looked back at Bhadra’s pause behind, then they turned towards Bhadra’s reaction and they smiled,

“Bhadra, are you amazed? Nice right? This is our school!” said Saagar,

A spectacle calm edifice with a beautiful green garden and a few unique flowers and Saagar walks back near the gate where Bhadra stood and holds his hand bit by bit walked inside the school looking at the garden,

As soon as they entered, students inside the school started to ask Saagar and Tapi,

"Who is this cute boy?"

Tapi is tired of introducing him as his cousin again and again, and on the other end Bhadra gets nervous looking at the crowd, he could see some students of his height and wish them with a bound smile but he couldn't lift his head for the tall students, many students loved him for his cuteness and squeeze his cheeks which is calming down his nervous system slightly.

"Bhadra, did you know even your mother and father studied in our school," says Tapi,

A slight shock reaction from Bhadra, Tapi lifted his left hand and holds it firmly, Saagar on the other end holding Bhadra's right hand and looking at Tapi,

"Dude what are you trying to do? He won't come with you do not force him to cry" said Saagar,

"I'll show you the classrooms of your parents where they studied," says Tapi,

"He is bluffing, if you come with me, I will take you to the amazing flying hills," said Saagar,

"Did you complete your homework today?" says Teacher,

All three turned behind, Bhadra is looking at a glossy polished brown shoe of a tall man, Saagar and Tapi looks at the Teacher,

“Yes, sir I have,” said Tapi,

“How about you,” asked Teacher,

“Sir....” Paused Saagar,

“Don't you know, I am coming to your classes today to check the assignments, The one who missed will stay in the class for the whole day and work on the assignments, then you all are allowed to the event, if not you will sit in the class alone!” said Teacher and leaves,

“Dude it’s showtime! You are in big trouble, forget flying hills, I don’t think you will at least come out of the class today, Run!” said Tapi,

Saagar’s happy face faded slowly, Tapi feels bad looking at drowning Saagar, removes his bag, and gave his assignment book to Saagar,

“We took a week to complete it, I don’t know how you will make it in a few hours dude, give it a try,” said Tapi,

Saagar leaves Bhadra's hand, grabbed the book from Tapi, and ran towards the classroom, Tapi took Bhadra the other way towards the high school building,

“This is where your parents pursued their high school,” says Tapi,

Both went to the second floor and Tapi points his hands towards a spot from the balcony,

“Are you able to see the chairs in the garden?” asks Tapi,

Bhadra saw a bunch of tall bamboo plants and tiny seaters beneath with the pair of glowing flowers next to it,

“That is where your parents and their classmates use to have lunch during break hours, this is the only tall building presented in our school compared to others, and you will be astonished by the view from the terrace, come let's go there,” says Tapi,

Both kept climbing to the terrace,

“Check this out, it’s called a library where you have plenty of imaginations sculpted inside a book which lets us travel into a different dimension of the world, similar to your drawing books Bhadra! Like you visualize a different world right... somewhat closer to it, few use colors to build their world and few with the words to build their universe, but I don’t think your father use to come for the library, might be your mother had visited” said Tapi,

Bhadra observed a few students inside the library, a ghost silently, without turning around some have lost themselves in the world of imagination, a silent image of sculpts, Bhadra kept looking at the readers,

“This is nothing, let’s go further come,” says Tapi,

And he pulls Bhadra, holding his hand, and began to move next floor,

“This is the place where your parents completed the final year, the entire row from here is the senior's classroom,” says Tapi,

There were many seniors present in the bay, unfortunately, Bhadra couldn’t see any of the tall students, he only heard the deafening sound from their classes including the row and the place was a complete mess with a weird noise, but a senior saw Tapi and Bhadra glancing their floor and he starts walking towards them, Tapi holds Bhadra hands firmly and sighs Bhadra to move out faster towards the terrace, by then the senior ran to them faster and caught the boys,

"Hey, you guys are primary students, right? Don't you know it is prohibited for you to come here? What are you doing here? You shouldn't be here without necessity, if you won't leave this place right now, I am going to take you to the principal" warns senior,

"I just came to show the top view to my cousin, can you please let us go to the terrace? Once done we will immediately leave this building" says Tapi,

"Why aren't you listening to me, come let's go to the principal right away!" says senior,

Senior drags Tapi's hand strongly, both had to move for the aggressive pull by him,

"Okay don't, please leave me, I will go back, I am sorry..." says Tapi,

Senior leaves Tapi's hand, disappointed Tapi slowly walks backward holding Bhadra's hand, and seriously staring at senior,

"Bhadra, don't worry! Without a miss I will show you the top view" says Tapi,

Both stepping down gradually from the high school building,

"Seniors will leave for their homes in the afternoon and return in the evening for the event, so the last floor will be free at noon, we will visit here with our classmates later," says Tapi,

No sad and no happy Bhadra getting down from steps normally with Tapi,

"This is primary student's world, even your parents have spent their primary classes from here when they were small babies like you," said Tapi,

Bhadra stood near the first-grade classroom and glancing the babies, a few are crying, a few are sleeping looked cute, a few turning the book pages plainly and a few sitting in a good style waving the book and creating wind for themselves for the high temperature in the classroom. Tapi diverts Bhadra pulling his hands towards his classroom. As soon as they entered the class Tapi saw students sitting next to the entrance at a desk staring at both, in the center of the classroom few girls were practicing something for the event and some other boys were busy with their entertainment playing head and bush from the coin, also few other girls were chit-chatting, and Saagar on one side of the corner busy writing the assignments, while glancing both marched towards a group of girls and Tapi introduced Bhadra to Hemavati, she is surprised looking at a cute boy Bhadra and walks towards him,

"Hi, cutie pie, what is your name?" asks Hemavati,

Bhadra is quiet, Hemavati doubtfully turned towards Tapi,

"He hasn't learned to speak yet, his name is Bhadra," says Tapi,

"Oh, I see... are you ready for the skit?" asks Hemavati,

"Yes, I am prepared," said Tapi,

"Then shall we rehearse once?" asks Hemavati,

"Sure," said Tapi,

Tapi lifts Bhadra and made him sit on the desk at the beginning row,

"From here you will be able to see them skit clearly!" says Tapi,

All other students were murmuring in the class and some rushed to stand in the front as soon as Hemavati and her team planned to rehearse,

"Stop, I haven't seen this act let me go forward," says a student to the pushers from behind,

Bhadra saw some of the students were messing up themselves, by then one of the members walked inside the classroom wearing a costume of a huge flower and sat in the center of the class rooming with a gorgeous smile, Hemavati entered in a magnanimous butterfly costume and seemed very beautiful as an angel, the audience in the class got amazed with the flair graces in the costume and everyone started to cheer them with the high spirited clap, butterfly in the garden flying for a while flapping its shiny wings dazzling with the nature's vitality, one with the moderate flap found a huge flower and gets closer to it, then the flower got up while a life approaching towards it,

"I am the king of this garden, and for all these flowers over here, I don't want strangers to be in my garden," says flower,

"I am the one destined as a constancy of your existence," says butterfly queen,

"Certain hopes of this destiny lead us to fade into the bags of dust, these bridges of existence and the survival never sailed towards the paradise, like some belief showered a lie as some hands offered the execution of our fate," said flower,

"Agonies in your sky are visible, but an everlasting united shield will blend in the history while the travelers connect from two different environs," says butterfly,

“Unsure destiny yet fades away as planned by the nature, why for someone's happiness?”

“That depends on your take on a theme, but the mortality is not in our buckets my friend,” said butterfly,

“Our friendship cannot happen just because nature had planned for us, right?” asks flower,

“Hey lovely flower, this friendship is an incarnation of your doubts and the achiever of your beautiful emotions to aid your sufferings,” said butterfly,

Flower got up and stares at butterfly with a tiny smile emerging from its petal,

“This friendship is from the heart which bonds for more than a word you hear,” says butterfly,

Flower smiled,

“Do you mean it?” asks flower,

"I could say, this friendship is the best plan from the divinity to its nature,” says butterfly,

“Scarcity upon the strangers in me will always be difficult to fade but it depends on how you would try being what you remark” asked flower,

Flower raised an inch higher

“But you seem better than the lives I trusted earlier, you are allowed here at any time!” says flower,

Butterfly queen with a glad impression propels a signal while the troop of tiny butterflies appears in the garden staging different color textures symbolizing an aura of heavens meeting the flower mistress confessed by a god itself, babies and few primary children entering with the tiny butterfly costume inside the classroom, everyone is amazed while also Bhadra's eyes were filled with a new visual aid, unexpected laughter roar entering the class, everyone turned... There comes TAPI...! In the devil costume, the ambiance of a dreadful dark wind while the devil crawling inside the garden and stepping up on smiling floras ends their life and intangible tears, whilst butterflies flicker from the devil's stomp.

Once upon a time in the world of heavens, a tornado carries the dark atmosphere with loads of negativity to test the potentiality of a few bonds between the soil and its nature while the weakened with strength lost control and the rage of the tornado turned more powerful for them to promise their breath and some were injured with a curse of sadness, the anticipation of a guardian to voice the sinner to fade him swiftly,

"Stop your annihilation!" voiced butterfly,

Like the dark wind entices the reinforcement, the devil comes closer to the butterfly queen,

"You are not supposed to harm the lives, this is a zone where survivors breathe," says butterfly,

The devil in silence, turned around gradually glancing the space,

"What made you come here and disturb our atmosphere?" asks butterfly,

"I am the king of shadows," said devil,

“I am the ruler of this place,” says Butterfly,

“From this day on, you all bow to me! You can’t act on your own as I am your prince” says devil,

“You have destroyed many lives already when entering this place, how can you be the prince of savior but sure of a destroyer,” says Butterfly,

“As time flies you will adapt to my way of rules, for now, I suggest you all leave the place immediately because leaving someone alive doesn’t exist in my policies,” says devil and walks away,

The flower looked at the butterfly,

“I think we should vacate the place instead of arguing with this monster it’s a betterment for us and our troop,” says flower,

Butterfly looks at the devil, flower staring at the helpless butterfly, turned back to flower with no words initiates a minute waveform generated from its antenna to its troop, the tiny butterflies in the field gradually comes back to its queen and assembled, butterfly turned to their troop and commands to find a new garden immediately. The tiny troops flew searching for a new environment, the devil on the other side walking back to its place observed all the butterflies flying upon him faster, he turns back and saw the butterfly queen still hovering in the garden in front of a flower, the devil kept looking at the butterfly for a long while then smiled and walks back to butterfly queen,

“Hey, I think you have something for me!” proclaimed Devil,

“What do you mean?” asks Butterfly,

“I heard those colors in your wings are alleged to be a luck if latched upon?” asks the devil,

“It is said to be a blessing,” said butterfly,

“Why don’t you bless me,” asks Devil,

“Bless you for?... To curse others?” asks Butterfly,

“To take care of you all,” says Devil,

“I apologize, it is the process of instinctive and they are not controlled by us,” said Butterfly

“I do have a great offer for you,” says devil,

“I am not expecting any kind of offer from you, nor we will accept it, please leave us alone Mr. Devil,” says butterfly,

“At least, listen to what I have for you?” asks Devil,

Butterfly and the flower looking at him without any reply,

“If you try the blessings thing from your wing, all of your troop can remain here without my interference!” says devil,

“That's so kind of you but thanks for the offer, we are already in search of a new garden and we are not interested in your dark jokes! Thank you once again” says butterfly,

Butterfly with a smile turned back and the flower indicated a big thumbs up to the queen but the devil on the other end seemed embarrassed then all of a sudden he took a big sword and vigorously cuts off the butterfly queen’s wing, students watching the activity in the classroom were in big shock, the butterfly queen on the ground shouting with pain in a very sharp voice, Devil walks closer to her,

"You rejected me and I disarmed you," says devil,

The team comes inside the classroom with a big cloth covering the act, a blinded act with a sharp sound that frequently approached from the cloths extremely and a few minutes later the team returned then takes off the cloth,

The Devil sitting upon a huge dead flower with full color on his body and butterfly queen on the other side with a wing cut, lying on the ground and all the color from its wings are faded to a spine wing, butterfly slowly turning to a pale color, a life that was assassinated by a sinner for its beautiful color who believed in absorbing its existence for serving himself an evil fortune,

Bhadra is looking at a butterfly lying on the ground with a little tear from its eye, breaking his heart with an immense feeling of suffering, meanwhile, he gets some flashes in his mind that took him to the flashback,

A heavy raining sound with a rare thunder strikes in the late evening, Yamuna teaching him the drawing and Bhadra is trying to scribble at a random point and his house main door opened slowly Bhadra and Yamuna turned towards the door, thunder filled dark sky outside heavy rain sounds that emerging and he saw a person stood in the darkness with a suitcase in hand near the door and a slight lighting strike behind him reveals the devil faced man who is standing without a movement and Bhadra gets scared looking at him then he jumped to hugs his mother but she smiles,

"Hey dear, Bhadra come to papa," says Krishna,

Father Krishna walks out of the darkness and entered inside,

Devil faced father walks closer to Bhadra and lifts him but Bhadra's scared intuit pressurize his heart to beat faster, flashback fades to the shadows and Bhadra comes back out of it,

A lying butterfly queen in the middle of the classroom... and the devil on the other end command other small butterflies to obey his order from now onwards, Bhadra feels strange about the uncontrollable situation, he got down from the bench, walks out of the class, a screeching dialogue from the drama of butterfly queen fading away while Bhadra walked out of the classroom,

"Mr. Devil, you did a mistake and which aroused the giant by cutting off our wings of life, you have disarmed your destiny!" says butterfly queen,

Bhadra skips the act by walking towards a small garden in front of the school, but Tapi saw Bhadra walking out of the class and he is unable to break out of the skit, he wanted someone to stop and take care of Bhadra while walking out, but Saagar was also busy writing his assignments and did not notice Bhadra walking out, Tapi's was helpless but still tried to manage to continue in the act, Bhadra on a with drowsiness in his head kept crawling on the grasses of the garden, blurred vision, he heard the voices of his mother,

This world was created by a balance of fire and water, and the life in it was planted in the lands of light and dark, the heart and minds in this land were always confused like the stars in between sun and moon disabled to judge who was rotating right and who is to the left.

"Bhadra!" shouts Tapi running on the grasses,

Bhadra sitting on a broken stone bench, looking at a yellow flower and tiny flies entering inside the petals and some rotating around it,

“What happened to you Bhadra? Why did you leave the classroom? Is anything wrong? Are you not well? Do you want me to take you back to the house or shall I get you the tablets given by your mom?” asks Tapi,

Bhadra looks at him silently and didn’t reply.

“Bhadra, please do not surprise me, let me know immediately if there is any kind of problem, I am unable to understand what you are going through from the inside!” says Tapi,

Bhadra kept turning back to the yellow flower,

“It seems you did not like the act... you should have stayed till the end, you have missed the main part of it,” says Tapi,

Small flies fighting to enter the yellow flower,

“It’s ok, you can watch the complete act in the evening on the stage, that would be more engaging,” says Tapi,

A strong wind arrived and all the tiny flies near the yellow flower flew away, but one fly remained inside the petals despite being secured from the wind blow, unfortunately, flower closed its petal and a fly stuck inside the flower,

“You can’t sit here all day Bhadra, we should be away from teachers noticing us, please walk with me, let us go to our class, it's lunchtime,” says Tapi,

World of a beautiful flower captures a two-winged survivor, but a viewer with an unknown spell in his feelings plucks the flower and releases the petal, Tapi lifted Bhadra upon his shoulder and takes him back to the classroom, while the fly stuck inside the flower did fly away, Bhadra takes the flower with him, Tapi saw him holding the flower,

"Bhadra, when an individual's need is fulfilled, there will be a big crowd waiting for their needs that depended on him, this is a cycle which keeps rotating," says Tapi,

Both entered the classroom and Bhadra looks at everyone opening their lunch box with a variety of color dishes from their houses, sharing the food with each, the happiness with their munch had an immersive bond with each other, Tapi and Bhadra walked near a big circle of students sitting and making fun of hiding someone's tiffin box and Tapi lifts his bag and takes out his box but Bhadra's lunch box was missing,

"Hey, who did it!" asks Tapi,

Everyone in the group with a stealer expression, Tapi is unable to identify the person who took Bhadra's tiffin box, Hemavati next to Bhadra kept smiling,

"Here you go, if you again leave class in the middle without informing me, this is how we will surprise you again and again Bhadra," says Hemavati and returned his tiffin,

Tapi smiled looking at Hemavati and took the box from her then opened it and gave it to Bhadra, a student named Cheyyar sitting next to Bhadra was looking at his box, then Bhadra offered his box to him, Cheyyar smiled and offered his plate to Bhadra mixed with multiple dishes bought from all the students at class, Tapi introduced Cheyyar to Bhadra, but Bhadra chewing food turns to Cheyyar did not reply anything but turned back and focused on the colorful dishes on his plates,

"Finally, I can see him smiling. Thank God," says Hemavati,

“I think, he is foody!” says Hemavati,

“Na, actually these things are new to him,” says Tapi,

Meanwhile, the drawing teacher Manimala entered the class,

“Students! All registered participants for the painting competition should assemble in section A with your paint boxes immediately!” said Manimala.

Few students in the class were having food, some chewing slowly and some staring at teacher Manimala, she looked at all the strange faces, Tapi looking at Manimala and chewing faster.

“Fine, participants come to the class once finished with your lunch!” told Manimala.

Tapi rapped his tiffin box inside the bag once done with his lunch, then checked for the paint box and also for his inspired Bhadra’s drawing book, and left the class. Within a few seconds, he walks back to Hemavati,

“Hemavati, can you take care of Bhadra until I return?” asks Tapi,

“Sure, no problem,” says Hemavati,

“And can you give him these tablets, once he finishes with his lunch, asks Tapi,

“Sure, I will, and all the best for you,” said Hemavati,

Tapi gets closer to Bhadra

"Hey, I will be back within half an hour you be with Hemavati she will take care of you!" says Tapi and left the class,

"Hey Tapi, All the best for your drawing competition, do well, said a few other students in the class.

"Thank you!" replied Tapi and rushed towards Section-A with his bag.

Bhadra finishes the lunch and kept his lunch box on the floor, Hemavati helped him keep his box in Tapi's bag.

"Saagar can you please open these tablets and help him feed, we will wash our tiffin boxes and return in a few minutes," says Hemavati,

"Ok try to come soon Hemavati!" says Saagar and she leaves the class with her buddies,

Crunching sound of tablet sheets, Saagar was trying to open the capsules, meanwhile Cheyyar behind

"Dude nobody is in the class now," says Cheyyar with a lot of excitement, and his eye enlarged,

A confused look by Saagar,

"This is the right time for us to leave the class... when nobody is around!" said Cheyyar,

"Oh yeah...! Now I wonder... I had some insecure feeling from the morning, now I realize that I am missing my cricket very badly today" said Saagar,

"Yeah... me too..." says Cheyyar happily

"Let's rock and roll!" says Saagar,

Saagar looks at Bhadra sitting quietly, and the tablet strip in his hands,

"Bhadra lets have the tablets in the playground, and then we will play cricket on the ground, what say?" asks Saagar,

Bhadra smiles at Saagar,

"Wow, this means you are ready I believe; boys pick up your things let's go!" says Saagar full of energy,

Bags were packed, each one of them is highly excited, one by one started to walk out of the class without making a noise, the gang formed near the door looking left to right to confirm if there is nobody outside, gradually one by one stepped out of the class, suddenly Saagar turns back!

"Dude, where are the bat, ball, and wickets? All seem to be in empty hands man? asks Saagar,

"Dude, it seems like none of them have carried from their home itself, since today we have college fest right," said Cheyyar,

"What to do then?" asks Saagar,

"Not to worry man, we will join random teams who are already playing in the ground," says Cheyyar,

Hemavati with her buddies laughing on some random topic and walking towards the classroom but she saw Saagar walking slowly like a thief outside the classroom, behind Cheyyar and Bhadra, she doubts their movement and shouted,

"Saagar...!"

The gang who is walking slowly got scared very badly and froze on spot for a moment, Saagar turned back and looked at Hemavati,

"Don't scream! We can hear you; we are going to wash our lunch boxes, wait in class for a few minutes, and we will return as soon as possible," said Saagar,

Everyone relaxed for a moment then took a deep breath and started to walk normally but they still had one obstacle to face,

"Buddy, how to cross the principal's chamber?" asks Cheyyar,

"Each one of us will cross his office in a few seconds of the interval," said Saagar,

Each one of them started to walk down the stairs and the next kid after a few seconds of the interval, Saagar, Bhadra, and Cheyyar behind murmuring,

"Saagar, do you think the principal will be there in the office right now?" asks Cheyyar,

"Maybe, may not be!" said Saagar,

Cheyyar did not understand Saagar's reply and then got up and started to walk in his turn, meantime without any interval Saagar grabbed Bhadra's hand and started to walk immediately behind Cheyyar, as soon as Saagar gets closer to the principal's office he looked inside and principal on a majestical chair staring at him oddly, yet Saagar did not stop and kept himself calm with a continuous walk, excited kids passing towards lower basement meanwhile a magical spirit called mood flying all around the school, unfortunately, found Bhadra and occupied in his humor which made him pressurize his footstep and laughs loud for no reason, Shocked Saagar looking at him and Cheyyar stepping down ahead turned back with a surprise and indicate Bhadra to be quiet.

“Bhadra?” hushed Saagar,

Bhadra started laughing again, Saagar with a helpless reaction on his face, drags Bhadra holding his hand firmly towards the end downstairs, however, Bhadra starts to increase his footsteps sound, and the scared gang started to rush out of the school building,

“Bhadra, please be quiet!” said Saagar and pulling him faster,

But Bhadra did not stop laughing but Saagar and Cheyyar got tensed, Saagar immediately commands his team,

“Guys this boy is gone mad! He is a laughing bomb now, who will blast his laugh now in a few seconds! Before we get caught by any of the teachers, let’s run to the ground as soon as possible...!” said Saagar,

Saagar holds Bhadra's hand and runs faster out of the school towards the ground, also the other students sprinted towards the ground breathlessly...

Boys breathing faster and looked at each other while the dust in the air flew towards them on the ground, some boys sat down to control their tiredness,

“Dude what is your problem? Why were you laughing so much?” Saagar questioned Bhadra

Bhadra with a smile looks at Saagar, Bhadra’s smile fades Saagar’s mind out of stress

“We would have joined you for laughing, any way you are free in this ground to laugh how much every you want,” said Saagar with a sudden change of his attitude towards the mess,

“Dude let’s request somebody to play on their team,” says Saagar to Cheyyar,

Cheyyar walks to a fielder on the ground,

“We are of seven members, can we join your team,” asks Cheyyar,

The unknown beautiful hearts at the ground agreed to play cricket with Saagar and Cheyyar, Saagar told Bhadra to sit on a small compound wall to have a look at their sports, and some eyes that are feeling happy, some hearts that feel fulfilled, and some zeal that empowering the activity in the stream of self, and some legs that have a strong bond with the ground of its universe, as like all times the vibrancy of entire enchants envisage in feast one’s eye on a soul hawking for the emotions veritable in its two eye sighting story of eccentric dimension. Every masterstroke from Saagar made their hearts beat out of happiness, Bhadra looks at happily jumping folks like a wing in their legs makes them float, a very next shot bowler knocks out Saagar from batting, and wicket jumps out a point with tons of depression that sadden few wings meanwhile Bhadra got down from the wall laughing intensely, Saagar walks to a player and gave his bat with an aura worried but he looked at Bhadra laughing and feels happy for being the reason for his very unique timing of happiness,

Tapi in drawing class arranged painting colors from his bag and drawing teacher Manimala started distributing empty sheets to fill their dreams, other students were already set with everything but Tapi is yet to dip his Painting brush into the ocean of colors,

“Theme for today’s drawing competition is nature!” says Manimala,

Students with no reaction cutely blinked their eyes,

“You all have seen the sunrise and sunset right, something like that or any kind of visuals you might have seen near your houses and school may be an amazing view you feel it is interesting, which should have made you surprised and unable to move out of that thought should be good for you to move that into your painting as creativity where your heart and vision accept to draw it!" says Manimala.

Tapi opened Bhadra's drawing book from his bag, he found the art of a boy inside the room with a lot of butterflies’, Tapi shakes his head left to right murmuring,

“Not a nature” murmurs Tapi,

Flips through the second page he saw boys sitting above the huge clock and they are tied to a thread linking to the watch and the butterfly hovering in front of them,

“Hmm no!” murmurs Tapi

Next, he found three boys walking in the street and a beautifully organized nature that passing dust with fire in the air,

“This is quite closer but not the exact one” murmurs Tapi and starts turning the pages faster,

While the paintings were traveling to the past, Tapi stops turning the pages and gets back to the previous one and got to see a painting that seems like the sketch of a small girl sitting on the lap of a person eating food in front of an injured butterfly, Tapi feels amazed by the dashing colors of the artwork and kept wondering

"How could he achieve this painting, I can't even replicate this," murmurs Tapi,

"Students have you decided? We don't have all day, your time starts now!" says Manimala,

Tapi again starts revolving the page faster and he feels some of them are complex to recreate but one art that engrossed him very much with its design, where the land of fire in which a lot of butterflies fluttering around where a revelation of wings caught up with fire in their wings, like always the sky wishes to be the mirror of earth emotions, and the blue sky filled with fire and the burnt wings of butterflies floating in the air alongside a huge smoke made this beautiful blue sky merge with gray smoke and a mild orange shade of sunset,

"Magnificent!" says Tapi,

Tapi gets amazed by the color tone of the painting done by Bhadra, he begins to examine the whole painting faster and closes the book while Manimala came closer to him gave the drawing sheets,

In other parts of this territory, Saagar and the whole team occupied a large tree by lying on separate branches like a resting bird after winning a couple of matches against the random team on the ground, meantime Cheyyar broke up a small branch from the tree and makes it into small pieces and throws them as disturbing their team from the restful sleep, tensed teammates started to pull Cheyyar legs above to them on forcing him to slip down from the tall tree,

"I wanted to inform you that we are simply wasting our time over here...! Let's go to flying hills...! Shouted Cheyyar while others forced him to slip from the tree,

Saagar turned towards Cheyyar,

"Correct, you always remind me the right things at right time, I like you!" said Saagar then pulled his legs harder to slip,

Cheyyar slipped! Other students receding slowly from the tree went paused for a moment looking at Cheyyar falling rapidly but somehow teammates at the bottom managed to catch him from getting hurt, Saagar got down and looks back at the tree some of them from the team remained lying on the branches as they refuse to join Saagar for trekking towards the flying hills and rest walked towards the bus stop, a very mild drizzle with cold wind slowly entering the small hearts made the journey to start motivationally peaceful for the gang at the bus stop,

"One of our teachers said that your parents are the ones who created the butterfly-devil skit and they specially mention their acting which is nevertheless to any of the performances in this entire town and none of the upcoming batches were able to accomplish it!" said Saagar to Bhadra,

Bhadra looking at Saagar with no expression!

"We also heard that whole town folks would come to our school fest to only watch your parents immersive acting in the butterfly-devil skit," said Saagar,

"They received the national award for spreading the best message, their skit photos are printed in school magazines every year," said Cheyyar,

Bhadra suddenly gets head pain and started crying sharply, while he gets some visual flashes of Saagar and himself flying in the air, he turns around at the moment both of them were sitting upon a huge butterfly with its powerful wing fluffing sound but Bhadra also found a fire that is burning rapidly below them in the beautiful land of hope, people and animals are blended with fire and they are looking at flyers with tear while they are in the hope of resurrection, to see the scream for help and the pain towards beloved preaches and Bhadra comes back to the present and saw Saagar and Cheyyar talking to him,

"Oh my god, what happened to you Bhadra?"

Cheyyar reminds Saagar of tablet,

"Wait a minute, gosh I forgot to give him his tablets," murmurs Saagar,

Saagar, opened his bag immediately picks up the tablet sheet and borrowed a bottle of water from a passenger next to them, and gave it to Bhadra to swallow,

"I am sorry dear Bhadra, it was my mistake that I forgot to give you the tablets on time, my bad, I am sorry as I mean it," says Saagar,

"Are you ok? Will you be able to trek with us?" asked Cheyyar,

Saagar turns to his friend Cheyyar,

"I shouldn't have brought him?" asks Saagar to Cheyyar,

Both left in an uncertain state but Bhadra turned towards Saagar and smiled, the power of his smile made Saagar relief but Saagar was still tensed on managing him to get onto the hilltop,

Bhadra smiled and was happy for a reason, he found a very good window seat watching rapidly passing trees, flowers that danced left to right, and the birds that chasing the bus faster but an unmovable hill with one particular view of it with blue-orange colored sky and it's top covered with full of clouds, Saagar comes closer to Bhadra,

“Look at the hill covered with a lot of clouds, that is called flying hills, we will be there today, above the clouds!” said Saagar,

Fascinated Bhadra wondering about the hilltop and its amazing form,

“Can we see the crowd today in flying hills?” asks Cheyyar,

“As usual we will have a lot of people over there, most of them come to the hills only for visiting the butterfly shop!” said Saagar,

“Once we reach, I will take you there...” said Saagar to Bhadra,

Bhadra is looking at Saagar strangely,

“Are we going to the butterfly shop? Wow...!” Said Cheyyar,

Saagar smiled and turned to Bhadra,

“Anything you buy there will be in a form of a butterfly, and I will buy you the butterfly chocolate,” said Saagar.

FLYING POTION OF LUCK

Those fingers that seem to have a strong bond with oil paints and shoes that are sprinkled with colors, feelings of thrives that are always echoed by the color of life, mansions that are filled with beautiful children moving their wands to introduce the best magic spells to this world, the energy of the colors come in the form of identity to the dreams that dealt by souls, step by step bounding spells form an artistic vision that connects to the different dimensions of the world beyond the space,

"Oh... Even this year it's only two participants for this competition, I am not sure why the students of this school are not interested in drawing" murmurs Manimala,

The painting created by Tapi is not up to the mark compared to its original sculpt of Bhadra, but it has its style of flavor,

"Tapi and Ashoka...! Have you completed it? Thirty minutes given time is now over, submit your paintings and you can leave to your respective classrooms immediately," said Manimala.

Hurried Tapi peeps at Ashoka's paint, but Ashoka found him looking at his paper,

"What buddy? You want to see?" asks Ashoka,

And shows his artwork to Tapi,

"What are you waiting for? Get down!" said bus driver,

Boys are looked at the bus driver without any words,

“This is flying hills!” shouts bus driver,

Boys got down from the bus immediately, then the bus left swashing dust storm on them, wiping specks of dust from their faces Saagar and Cheyyar turned towards the iconic visual of flying hills in front of them, a very cold breeze waving downwards from the hills, boys started to rub their hands to warm up, wherein Bhadra is trying to lift his head but a severe neck block stopping him and he could able to see the mid part of the green hill,

“Guys let's run,” says Cheyyar,

“That’s not necessary we will walk with ease, we need to reach the hilltop together right, so let’s walk slowly together,” said Saagar,

Art of the devil holding a sword in front of eyes tied butterfly behind the hill with a moon nearing to them,

Tapi Looks at Ashoka’s paint and gets amazed, he looks back to his drawing and goes through for changes in his painting,

“Are you done?” asks Ashoka,

“Yes, almost!” replies Tapi looking at his paint,

“Show me yours,” asks Ashoka,

“Don’t worry you will lose today!” says Tapi with a sarcastic smile,

Tapi got up and handed over his painting to the teacher and walks with Ashoka, trying to seek the secret of getting the first prize for all these three years,

"Your painting was amazing, where do you get this amazing inspiration from?" asks Tapi,

"I imagine and always try to create new on my own," said Ashoka,

"Oh, I see...!" says Tapi.

"Boys you can't reach the hill by just walking, it's not as easy as you think, get inside my vehicle! I will take you up there in minutes, for each it is twenty bucks only!" says Jeep driver,

"We cannot even afford that uncle! We are left with a small budget reserved for shopping!" says Saagar,

"Hey boy's water bottles at just 5 bucks, it costs more than gold up there, buy it here! Why pay high at hills? Be brave!" said water bottle seller,

Boys kept moving with no response,

"You are going to regret once reached!" says shopper,

Boys yet did not care,

"We don't have enough money guys, so keep walking," said Saagar,

After a few meters from the entrance, they got to see a flex board which had a map with a lot of instructions and details about flying hills,

"Did you guys see that? Seems like there are a lot of things for us to see" told Saagar,

Bhadra was able to look at the bottom section of the flex board, which consist of small photos of mouthwatering dishes, Cheyyar kept wondering at the huge butterfly statue behind a glowing stone,

“Dude, do you know what it is?” asks Cheyyar pointing towards the board,

“That is the museum of different butterflies,” says Saagar,

“Oh, I see, how about this one?” asks Cheyyar,

“That’s a butterfly farm, come let’s start to go, we are already late,” said Saagar,

“Wow, Butterfly farm? We will go there without a miss” said Cheyyar,

“Butterfly farm is prohibited since they breed a variety of butterflies and they have to maintain cleanliness inside and to protect them from harmful viruses that are exposed most by public visits, hence visitors are not allowed,” said Saagar,

“Oh,” said Cheyyar with a low tone of voice,

“I have been there once,” told Saagar,

“Seriously? How come?” asked Cheyyar,

“Do you know Ashoka from our class?” asks Saagar,

Yes...

“His father works on that farm, he took us inside last year,” says Saagar,

“Did you see, how the butterflies grow?” asks Cheyyar,

“Yes! I have seen, but it takes time to form but the way it evolves to a butterfly is just celestial” said Saagar,

“Can you insist Ashoka, to take us once... please...” asks Cheyyar,

“Sure!” said Saagar,

“Great, dude...! What else is special inside?” asks Cheyyar,

“Once you enter the farm, you could see some butterflies laying eggs on plants and branches, some of the eggs are already hatched from that we could see the caterpillar introduced to this world, then those caterpillar starts eating their eggshell, and later feed themselves with leaf's and gradually continues, also the caterpillar sheds its skin to grow, over the time of period it eats so much so that the caterpillar becomes big enough, later caterpillar stops eating and hangs in a safe place like a branch or below the leaves then forms a protective layer around it while they call it as a chrysalis,” says Saagar,

“Chrysalis means?” asks Cheyyar,

“I am not sure, self-protected caterpillar forms as pupa, a very hard layer something like a stone an energy inside, this stage of pupa undergoes a lot of changes from within, fifteen days later a stellar that unfurl as the beautiful butterfly that emerges out of the chrysalis, but do you know the butterfly approach to this world with very small wings, with a fluid in its hands they wipe their wings to make it revive, strong and helps to expand in few minutes like a flower blooming faster, once the wings become strong and large they will be good enough to fly and add the beauty to the wind, these are the series of beauty called metamorphosis,” said Saagar,

“Wow, how did you know all these men?” asks Cheyyar,

“Villagers in farm thought me,” said Saagar,

“I think, due to this much information in your head, you are not able to concentrate on the math exam that you failed last week! Ha-ha-ha...” said Cheyyar and laughed,

“Nonsense I tried to make a note of it so that I could circulate the interesting thing to the entire school!” said Saagar,

“When are you doing that?” asked Cheyyar,

“I have already given those notes to Hemavati, I will ask her to give them to you, also our Tapi has drawn the butterfly cycle colorfully on the very first page,” said Saagar,

“I do remember that Tapi was doing something on your notebook during class hours,” said Cheyyar,

“Yeah, exactly!” says Saagar,

Suddenly a big jeep from the hilltop propels toward Bhadra horning heavily and the vehicle sound hurried, Saagar saw the jeep coming over Bhadra, by the time jeep gets closer to Bhadra, Saagar quickly catches his hands then pulls him aside, aggressively rapid vehicle passes very next to Saagar and a breathless moment made the boys very silent spectators, boys stunned on the spot for few seconds, Cheyyar turned back to the jeep... tourist inside the jeep appeared to be negatively insane, tossing lighted crackers on the road, some of them are creating the smoke out of their mouth holding the burnt paper roll and some holding a glass bottle in their hands, Cheyyar turned back slowly towards the gang, Tapi makes Bhadra sit aside and gives him the water bottle, Bhadra like a frozen doll with little sweat drank the water,

"Are you okay Bhadra?" asks Saagar,

"Dude let him walk in the safe lane," says Cheyyar,

Some jeeps slowly returned from the top, Cheyyar looked up for the crossroads sharply, jeep turned in the short road bends in the edges, gradually comes closer to the boys by then everyone ran towards the corner of the road and paused for a while then started walking after the jeep passed, some of the jeeps do come faster and some at a slow pace...

"Hey, guys...! Please be aware that this hill has a tricky road, I have heard negative stories about it, try to be alert of any vehicle sound you hear, when you sense be quick to keep yourself aside until they pass" said Saagar,

Sweating Cheyyar had a silent look at Saagar,

"Dude why didn't you inform us about these things earlier, I wouldn't have joined you, shall we go back?" asks Cheyyar,

"Don't worry, I am there to take care of you! You just follow my orders and that's enough!" said Saagar,

"You seriously are a mystery box today, with a lot of surprises," said Cheyyar,

"I was about to tell you but your questions diverted me!" said Saagar,

Cheyyar and Bhadra looked unusual and they are checked at the bottom of the hill wondering at jeeps passing towards the exit" Saagar noticed two worried faces,

“Guys, even I have to return home safely, come let's go…” said Saagar,

“Yeah, you are there right now, but not while my father thrashing me,” says Cheyyar,

“Buddy listen to me, forgot to tell you the main thing, when I visited the butterfly farm, the villager told me a very interesting thing,” said Saagar,

“Again…” says Cheyyar and turned towards Saagar,

“The villager told me that butterflies decide the color for their wings and it is so clever that they do design it at the stage of pupa when they are inside the shell, and that color from its wing represents a message to other butterflies to conclude that it belongs to certain territories, especially in the day time, and there is one special butterfly which is in blue color that is commonly recognized as the rarest creature in the planet because of its true blue colored wings because all other blue creature in the earth make their color with microscopic structure and not even a single creature in the earth makes blue pigment for itself, the one and only butterflies has cracked the code for making the true blue pigment of its form,” said Saagar,

Rapidly Bhadra turned towards Saagar and starred,

“Whatever you explained was so much confusing, I understood that colorful butterflies do belong to one territory and the blue one is special, that’s it right!” asks Cheyyar,

“I tried so hard to explain you, and you just got it partially not bad!” responded Saagar,

"I'm too confused with this concept but I've just been informed by villagers inside, where I can share them with my understood perspectives," said Saagar,

After some time, there were no vehicles and the quiet mountain seemed haunted, boys do feel scared and they try to push themselves faster to the top, suddenly a vehicle came soundlessly at a ghost paced speed, the boys were too fast to keep themselves aside while being experienced for a while,

"Guys, this is the spot! Our seniors once met with an accident, please walk carefully!" said Saagar,

"What happened to them," asks Cheyyar,

Saagar gets irritated with his rain of questions,

"Dude if I told you, what happened to them! How vigorous that accident was! I believe it will break your sleep for tonight! And it becomes a big nightmare for you, please stop asking questions" said Saagar,

The art of scare does shape them slowly,

"Do you feel any changes?" said Cheyyar,

"This amazing green, right!" said Saagar,

"No, when we entered this hill, there was an amazingly positive vibe with us, but now there is a negative smoke occupying us drastically," replies Cheyyar,

"I did not find any difference!" said Saagar,

"Are you sure?" asks Cheyyar,

"Stop overthinking," says Saagar,

Boys kept walking in silence which is graying their minds, stressed out sweat and physical tiredness make them feel like giving up, Saagar who kept moving forward with confidence even while exhausted which motivates others to push themselves hard,

Finally, they could see a mini stall aside with water bottle crates outside, with some snack packets but wretched timing of the shopkeeper closing the stall and loading the water bottle into the crates and arranging them inside the stall, frightened boys rapidly ran towards the shop shouting,

"Don't close the shop, sir…!" shouted Saagar,

"Hey…! Wait…!" said Cheyyar,

One after another reached to shopkeepers asking for,

"Do you have water to drink sir?"

The shopkeeper waits for all the boys to gather one by one after running, then he gave them a huge water jar, Cheyyar grabs it to feel the cold temperature around the jar and feels the energy restoring, Saagar grabs the jar from him and started to drink, later they passed each other after their turn of loading their stomach with sweet-tasting water, shopkeeper asks them,

"You should have taken the Jeep," said Shopkeeper,

"We have a very less money," said Saagar,

"Without any elders with you?" asks Shopkeeper,

"Yeah!" said Cheyyar,

"And you are late to the hills, it's very dangerous boys!" Said shop keeper and,

Starts loading the goods lying outside the shop and he closes the stall and waited in the road with a heavily loaded bag behind him,

"Can you tell me what is the time, right now?" asked Saagar,

"Maybe 4:20 pm..." says Saagar,

"Hey, it's already closing time!" said shopkeeper,

Boys looked at each other's worried faces,

"I suggest you guys go back to the houses and return with your parents tomorrow..." said shopkeeper,

He stops a jeep coming from the hilltop and gets into it and he also asked boys to get inside the jeep with him,

Refused boys, wished to move ahead and the shopkeeper left the hill, a sarcastic smile that found in boys but a serious eye that haunt by choice, a lot of tenses that hound inflow but they had to rest as they seem to be too low, mindsets that are confused on negative blow but the goal that is set spoke them to as-is flow,

"What are we going to do now? He says it's already too late..." said Cheyyar,

"Moving with this speed is our fault, we should have paced a little faster," said Saagar,

"Chit-chatting that killed our time! You started a big history on the roads" said Cheyyar,

"Brother, you are the one who asked for it, I thought of making this journey a little bit interesting with some unique stories so that we cannot feel the tiredness..." said Saagar,

"We could have done that by walking faster also dude!" Said Cheyyar,

"Things happened, now what's next? Are we sticking to the plan or heading backward like a scared puppy?" asks Saagar,

Saagar is still Confident, but he feels like losing it cause of the team is a little worried and everyone sitting aside in silence, meanwhile, Saagar looks at Bhadra standing in front of him,

"Dude, I am sorry, I couldn't take you to the hilltop this time, hope so... next time we will!" said Saagar,

However, Bhadra is looking at something else behind Saagar, Cheyyar looks at the jeep passing downwards,

"Did you see something? No jeeps are passing from the entrance now, I think shopkeeper was right, it is closing time up there!" said Cheyyar,

"If we did hire a jeep at the entry we would have reached very long back and by this time we would have completed our shopping and returned to school, anyway let's go back to at least watch the shows," said Saagar,

Then Saagar got up and turned around, walked alone for a few steps downwards, then turned back checking out for the boys with him and it seemed like Bhadra and Cheyyar left at the same spot refusing to go backward, Saagar walks back to them with a surprise,

"Unbelievable, you guys are ok to walk to the hilltop?" asks Saagar with a smile,

Surprise faced Saagar walks closer to Cheyyar and looks at him then turned towards Bhadra, looking at Bhadra constantly his reaction fades to normal, Saagar walks gets closer to Bhadra and found that Bhadra was busy looking at something on the vast green hill,

"What are you looking at Bhadra?" asks Saagar and tried to analyze the green mountains around him,

Then he looks at Bhadra's viewpoint and he realizes that Bhadra was looking at the entrance,

"Hey dude, what are you looking at? That's the place where we came from! Its entrance" said Saagar and points his finger,

"See that is where we got down in the bus and do you see that? A big gate, that's the entrance gate" says Saagar,

But Saagar discovered that Bhadra focusing on something else, Saagar with his microscopic eye began to glance meticulously and a couple down the hills holding each other's hand and conversing, Saagar and Cheyyar peeking,

"Dude isn't there anyone apart from those lovers down there?" asks Cheyyar,

"How do I know? I could see the same as you!" says Saagar with curiosity,

The couple standing in front of the firewood, guy gets closer to the woman and puts his hand on her shoulder then she smiles with a lash of love, together they step ahead to the firewood and stretched their arms towards the fire and the woman keeps her hand on cheek and smiles while getting themselves warm and the guy inhales and exhales a very long breath, while the guy exhale the breath a huge amount of smoke comes from his mouth women looked at it and laughing, but their face is not visible for the boys as they are looking from the mid part of the hills, Cheyyar turns back to Bhadra and Saagar but they seem to be tied down looking at the couples down there, Cheyyar slowly walks back without disturbing them and he picked up a stone and throws it to the lovers at the bottom that even disturbs Saagar and Bhadra then Saagar turns to Cheyyar,

"Hey, dude? What are you doing?" yelled Saagar,

Saagar turns back to the couple at the bottom of the hill, couple were looking at the sky and wondering at the stones that flying toward them, Saagar and Cheyyar looked at their confusing act and started laughing, the couple again stretched their hands in front of the firewood to warm themselves then Cheyyar feels to throw the stones again, he picks up a stone and walks few steps backward and gets full energy from within and runs pulling his hands behind holding a stone and gives a rush through his arm swinging towards the bottom of the hill but the stone just lost its direction and flew away in a small range,

"Dude, that's not a good throw at all, watch me," said Saagar,

Saagar searched for a lightweight stone with a flat design,

"You should choose your stone properly first," said Saagar,

He stood at the edge of the hill without moving he just swings his arms with moderate energy, rotating fan alike stone reaches closer by to the couple, Cheyyar went and bought the similar stone as Saagar chose, Cheyyar stood at the end of the hill curve and throws with the full energy, it went close but did not reach them, Saagar and Cheyyar started to find flat-surfaced stone in their surroundings and kept throwing but none of the throws reached the couples, for some stone that went and hit them yet again tried looking at the sky, also to their left and right, Bhadra standing in the silence like always and kept looking at the couple's, Saagar kept trying in different ways to throw, Cheyyar tried in his way,

“Dude when your target is at the lower level, your throw might travel only for a few meters and it drops,” said Saagar,

Cheyyar looks at Saagar confusingly,

“Instead, you have to throw the stone in medium height,” says Saagar,

“Exactly what height?” asked Cheyyar,

Lift your hands to your shoulder level” said Saagar,

“Okay, wait, let me try once!” said Cheyyar,

He lifts a very light stone with a fine flat surface,

“Dude, look at this stone, should this be fine right?” asks Cheyyar,

“Yeah, this stone should travel a good distance, throw it!” says Saagar,

Cheyyar takes the position and lifts his hand towards the sky once,

“Dude not that much height,” says Saagar,

“Wait let me stretch once,” said Cheyyar and brings his arms down to the shoulder level,

Pulls back his hands in full of energy he releases the stone at the edge of the hill, the stone passes very faster only for few meters, and started rotating in the air marching towards the destiny, Cheyyar connected with his beautiful energy floating in the air alike ocular of an eye, however guy with the women saw the stone flying towards them and catches as soon as the stone gets closer to the women’s eye, the guy found the kids stood at the curve looking at them and they are preparing to throw another stone, the women waves the hand towards the kids at the top,

After Cheyyar finishes throwing, Saagar behind him is ready for his turn, Saagar ran towards the edge of the curve and gives one more throw of his,

“Dude, I think even this stone travels well,” said Saagar after completing his throw,

Cheyyar near the edge of the hill says,

“Dude, stop...!” said Cheyyar and looks at the couples after his throw,

By the time Cheyyar stops him, he was finished with his throw which cannot be undone, the white marble stone rotating faster than a fine throw yet ranking at miles with an unstoppable rotation,

“What a superb throw! A stone with wings!” said Cheyyar,

Couples spot the stone approaching towards them and the guy steps in front staring at the boys standing in the curve of the hill, stone rotated above him that cleaves the firewood and some woods arranged in the fire blown out for the hit, Saagar and Cheyyar are left at shock looking at the stone hitting firewood, Saagar looks at Bhadra in shock to see his reaction then Bhadra eye reflects the lovers running away from the fire that caught nearby to them, Cheyyar calls Saagar waving from right hand to his shoulder by opening his mouth, Saagar comes out of Bhadra eye and views down towards the couple and they were running away from it and Cheyyar looks at Saagar and Saagar turned towards Cheyyar with a shock opening their mouths and Cheyyar turns back slowly towards lower hills and saw the fire that is spilled out causing a sensitive fire creating a small spark in the flying hills,

Tapi at the school lobby walking side by every section, while he passed ahead from his class to fill his water bottle, doubtfully he steps back in reverse to his class door and found the empty classrooms, at the moment he stood in the spot at the unexpected shock,

Downhearted boys for throwing a stone at a couple like a dark cloud forming above them and there comes a stupendous thunder, lights up the sky and also the hill, boys looked up and the soundless clouds few meters above them moving silently, boys opened their mouth and wondering at clouds upon them,

"Guys it's going to rain now! I think we should run to the hilltop immediately" said Cheyyar,

"Leave about rain, we could get hit by thunder you idiots, run!" said Saagar and drags Bhadra's hands,

Boys started to run in at the center of a road, another strong thunder striking the hill with a magnanimous flash that glared at the hill with higher brightness, and boys close their ears and kept running,

"Run faster!" said Saagar,

Cheyyar, Saagar, and Bhadra ran faster, Bhadra kept inhaling back-to-back and feels his leg getting shattered, sweat dropping in front of his eye, and his surrounding seems to be waving backward like dizziness causing him to fly, Bhadra looked at the hill at the front understood an immense obstacle they could encounter, one from the behind, another seems to be the last one from within,

Tapi stood looking at the empty class entrance expecting Bhadra and other classmates, unforeseen thunder struck behind him, then he ran towards the outer view of the school and looked at a huge lighting chain slowly moving from one end to another, his eye following the continuous lighting movement in the sky which is brightening up the entire mountain with white-blue light,

"How come people up there do survive, gosh!" murmurs Tapi in his mind,

Moderately slowed themselves while boys are tired of running through the zig-zag roads, the grey guy in the sky seems to be crawling slowly and forms enormously an absence of unexpected thunders, Saagar and Cheyyar bend themselves holding their knees and breathing heavily looking at each other's face Saagar seemed to be worried,

"I must have not thought you to throw the stones man!" says Saagar and inhales faster,

"Your throw was ultimate, it traveled so far and directly into the firewood buddy, amazing," says Cheyyar,

"I am afraid for doing it, and you are appreciating it?" asked Saagar,

"Don't worry, anyways the fire spilled out down there will be turned off by this rain that going to come now" says Cheyyar and looked up,

Saagar turned back slowly,

“Hey, where is Bhadra?” asks Saagar,

Cheyyar looking up turns back immediately with a shock,

“You were holding his hands, right?” Ask Cheyyar,

“Oh god, what have I done,” asks Saagar himself,

“Cool... Don’t worry he might have got tired and stood back somewhere here, come let's go back and bring him,” says Saagar and both ran back in the zig-zag roads,

Bhadra Inhales and exhales faster and wipes sweat with his tiny cute hands, few seconds later he walks aside and sat on a stone at the edge of the curve, a cold breeze wind is letting him calm down, then he looked at a deep down of the hill bottom something like a mysterious silence talking to him again a mystifying sound from the other side of the bottom hills, Bhadra turns to his left, a big tree that is burning makes a huge noise while falling, some animals screaming, and some silence that is preaching, Bhadra gets scared then lifted himself and looked around in the forest seeking for the help but unhappier empty roads and its negative energy attracting him more alike a ghost spectating him with a cloud of invisible dust, Bhadra starts walking in the unforeseen path.

DROP OF TRIFLING FRONTIER

Thoughts that lead one to perceive love, some thoughts that escort the shallow holding in a breath of closer ones, thoughts that bear someone's oppressions, and some that crawl in the roads of repulsion, Bhadra's father Krishna walking towards the house, worrying about his financial crisis for the survival of his beautiful family, as soon as he entered the gate, the door seemed to be locked and he gets closer for the confirmation and found that his wife and son were not present at home, Krishna set back himself aside near steps and started checking for pending office files, an hour later Krishna completes glancing his office files and turned back to the entrance and expecting for his family to return by then he feels too hungry but no one turned up, He got up tiredly and walks out to find some food for himself with slight stress and anger.

The craving that loaded with a couple of expectations, for the survival that being helpless with the parcel of aggression, the life that always entails its fulfillments but a situation which always kept the love with hunger, a few minutes later Krishna returned and found the doors which seemed to be open, removed his shoes then entered looking around for his wife Yamuna meanwhile he heard some noises from the kitchen, Krishna walked towards the kitchen and saw Yamuna was preparing food for him,

"Where the hell were you all this time?" asks Krishna,

"I had been to the groceries store," said Yamuna,

“I waited for hours!” said Krishna,

Yamuna did not respond anything, Krishna in anger looked around the kitchen and saw the vegetables,

“Where is Bhadra?” asked Krishna,

“Tapi took him to the school annual function. Even I am going there in another twenty minutes with my sister,” said Yamuna,

“What the universe with that culprit?” asks Krishna,

“Please respect, it’s my sister!” said Yamuna,

“All day you keep roaming, and you have a good reason for it, why don’t you be at home?” asked Krishna,

“Am I Roaming? Can’t you see, I've been to the store, you should give me some freedom, seriously!” asked Yamuna,

“I am not bothered about your freedom, it’s me waiting out of the house for a long time and you don’t turn up, so now you are not going anywhere stay at home!” said Krishna,

“Why shouldn’t I?” asked Yamuna.

“Because I don’t want you to roam all day, and there is nothing you have prepared to eat, why don’t you give a holiday for your roaming plans?” asks Krishna,

“Don't you understand, I need to bring Bhadra and Tapi from the school” said Yamuna,

“See this is just another reason, ask your sister to bring both,” said Krishna,

Accidentally a plate dropped down in the kitchen, it makes a clumsy noise, Krishna misunderstood and thought Yamuna intentionally threw the plate in anger for stopping her from going out, Krishna got up from the chair in anger walked inside the kitchen, and pulled her hands then slapped tight,

"I don't want your attitude in my house," said Krishna and looked at her aggressively,

"What is that sound," asked Tapi's Mother Netravati from the entrance of the house,

Yamuna with tears and Krishna walked out of the kitchen and looked at Netravati entering inside,

"I know, you have slapped my sister," said Netravati,

"Some people deserve the replies on the face," said Krishna staring Netravati seriously,

"Why do you torture my sister, it's a proof today," says Netravati,

"She is the actual problem," says Krishna,

"How can she? When the whole universe knows that you are a big drunk" said Netravati,

"What did you just say?" asks Krishna,

"Yes! Everyone about your house does gossip in this village, we lost respect because of you in our family" said Netravati,

"I don't care what others talk about my family, they would anyways talk for every nonsense things!" said Krishna,

“Do whatever you want but I am warning you! Next time you try something like this, I am going to get all the villagers to your house and you face the serious consequences!” says Netravati,

“I am scared right now!” replied Krishna,

“We are going to get our children now, I am going to take her with me, you can't stop us!” said Netravati,

“You know what... get lost both of you!” said Krishna and went to bed,

Netravati walks to Yamuna and wipes her tear and hugged her,

“One day... everything will be fine! Come let's go” said Netravati,

Netravati and Yamuna ran towards the bus stop,

Tapi wondering at the flying hills and recalled a dialogue of Saagar committing of taking Bhadra to the flying hills, his voice driving around in Tapi’s mind back-to-back, he gets a little tense,

“I cannot be calm right now, I need to find Bhadra” Tapi murmurs Himself and runs around the school,

Tapi found Hemavati at the entrance of the school with her friends conversing, Unfortunately, Bhadra was missing from their batch, so Tapi rushed towards Hemavathi,

“Where is Bhadra? I told you to take care of him, right? What happened?” asks Tapi,

“Tapi I am sorry dude, that idiot Saagar told me that he would wash his lunch box and return in five minutes but they haven’t turned up yet!” said Hemavati,

Tapi gets afraid,

“I saw him taking Cheyyar and Bhadra along with him,” says Hemavati,

Helpless look from Hemavati,

“I am not sure where they were heading to,” says Hemavati,

Tapi looked at the flying hills and turned back to Hemavati,

“Did you spot them anywhere outside?” asks Tapi,

“No, they just disappeared,” said Hemavati,

“I need to arrange the accessories for the skit, so I will not be able to join you, please don't mind,” said Hemavati,

“It’s okay I will go... search for them!” said Tapi,

“I couldn’t go near the playground, can search there?” asks Hemavati,

“Sure, I will right away,” said Tapi,

“Wait...!”

She gave a couple of entry tickets to the scary house,

“Try to return by fifteen minutes,” said Hemavati with a gorgeous smile,

Tapi is clean bold looking at her smile and the butterfly with the sparkles sprinkling in his stomach flying around with lots of happiness,

“Sure, I will be back soon,” says Tapi and ran towards the playground,

Bhadra walking with tears filled in his eye and the cold breeze pushing him backward like his parents wishing him to be safe, the feeling of missing his friends in the middle of the flying hills pushes him ahead, grey cloud above him suppresses the hill darker, screaming voices that are echoing slowly from the upper hills,

Tapi enters the playground but he couldn’t find any of his classmates, he walks to the random cricketers on the ground,

“Hi, did you find any of our classmates over here,” asks Tapi,

“From the morning there are lot many students who are joining us and later they leave but we are not sure to recognize exactly to whom you are looking for,” said Random player at the ground,

Ashoka enters the playground, found Tapi, and walks toward him,

“Dude, what are you doing here? Come let’s go to the scary house!” says Ashoka,

“No dude I am not coming,” said Tapi,

“It's starting in a few minutes now! Let’s go!” says Ashoka,

“I can’t until I find my cousin,” says Tapi,

"Oh, you are still searching for him?" asks Ashoka, turning left and right on the ground,

Afraid Tapi with low tone,

"Yes!" says Tapi,

"Did you check in all the sections?" asks Ashoka,

"Yes, everywhere I did!" said Tapi,

"How about Hemavati? Did you ask her?" says Ashoka,

"Yeah, she told Bhadra was with Saagar and they promised to return in five minutes but they did not!" says Tapi,

"Hmmm... Then your cousin will be with Saagar right!" said Ashoka,

Suddenly Tapi turned towards the flying hills,

"Oh my gosh! That stupid has gone," says Tapi,

"What happened...!" asks Ashoka,

"He was excited to take Bhadra along with him to the flying hill," said Tapi,

"Holy truth...!" says Ashoka looking at the flying hill,

"It's seeming too cloudy over there," says Ashoka,

Tapi looks at the flying hills and gets more worried,

“Our parents are going to come in another one hour, I don’t know what to answer them!” says Tapi and closes his face with two of his hands and breathes heavily,

“Dude, don’t panic...! nothing to worry about, seems they have been to hills long back, so by the time your parents reach here, boys would return!” says Ashoka,

“It will take a lot of time for them to reach the hilltop buddy, I don’t think they would return in an hour,” says Tapi,

“They cannot climb also, why because it’s the closing time! They can if they get a Vehicle and return fast” says Ashoka,

“You know Saagar and Cheyyar right...! They are very irresponsible!” says Tapi,

“Yes, but they are not so inhuman as you think, do not worry buddy,” says Ashoka,

“My cousin Bhadra has a lot of health issues, he doesn’t speak much, and you heard the huge thunder sound from the hilltop right!” says Tapi,

“Trust me, it's closing time over there, did you see the darkness, they should have got scared and by now they might have started to travel back to the school,” says Ashoka,

“That Saagar won’t!” says Tapi,

“Fine but you know there will be a lot of tourists...! They will help these guys, don’t worry, nothing is going to happen! Come with me” says Ashoka and takes Tapi along with him,

Worried Tapi walks to the school as soon as he entered, and both spot a huge crowd of students standing in front of the scary house, Tapi and Ashoka walk toward the queue,

“Tapi...!” screamed Hemavati,

Hemavati standing at beginning of the queue waving hands toward Tapi, both walked towards her,

“Did you find Bhadra?” asks Hemavati,

“I couldn’t find them, we both guessed it right, Saagar took Bhadra to the flying hills...!” says Tapi,

“What...? God...! How dare they did go out of the school without anybody’s permission,” says Hemavati,

“Shush... Silence... make it low... Let’s not spread it, even Bhadra is with them... so...” says Tapi,

“Hmmm... Okay let it go... join us in” says Hemavati pointing towards the scary house entrance,

Tapi stepped behind her and joined the queue, other students started yelling at Tapi for entering in between and not maintaining the queue order,

“No problem...! Close all of your mouths...” said Ashoka and even he joins the queue,

Saagar and Cheyyar have returned near the entrance of the hills without Bhadra, Cheyyar breaths heavily and looks back at the hill which is now half-covered with grey clouds around it,

Cheyyar turned towards the flex board next to him and saw the hill photo upon it,

"This should have been enough for us! Hill looks so amazing in this photo itself, why did we go up there to look at the same hills which are already available here!" says Cheyyar,

"Dude, stop it! Where is Bhadra?" asks Saagar,

"I did not find him anywhere until we return to the bottom here," says Cheyyar,

"We can't go back to the house until we find him!" said Saagar,

"Dude I cannot walk again to the top! I am done! You should search for him now" says Cheyyar,

"We have to go up and bring him back, we have no choice!" says Saagar,

"I will wait for you both here," says Cheyyar,

"I am not letting you sit!" says Saagar,

A great noise near the entrance of the hill, Saagar and Cheyyar kept silent for a second and looked at each other, noise that popped a few meters away from them, both walked towards the entrance gate and found a huge tree that caught up with fire lying upon the gate,

"Dude, it has blocked our way!" said Cheyyar,

Saagar looked at the huge gate with wall and steel cages covered to the exit of the hill,

“Are this wall and cage continuing all-corner of the hills?” asked Saagar,

“No, seriously I don’t know this amazing trap,” said Cheyyar,

Confused Cheyyar walked left and right to find the exit from the hills,

“Dude isn’t this stone we threw from up there?” asks Cheyyar,

Saagar looked at it and gets confirmed but he grabs the stone from Cheyyar and throws it away,

“Yes, brother this is the spot where the lovers stood with firewood,” says Saagar,

“Don’t tell me that, we are the reason for this huge magma here” says Cheyyar,

Saagar looks at the huge fire roaring around them and turned back to Cheyyar... hits on his head,

“I am hundred percent sure that you are the one responsible for this madness,” said Saagar,

Burning tree raising like a fire wave, meanwhile Saagar saw a van passing in front of the gate, boys ran shouting towards the gate,

Hello...!

Sir...!

Stop...!

Please...!

Help...!

Atrai stops the van after looking at a huge burning tree fell upon the gate meanwhile, he heard kids screaming from the inside seeking the help but he was unable to find anyone, a worker inside the van located the boys inside the gate and helps the Atrai to identify them, Atrai looked thoroughly inside the flame and rushed towards the gate along with his workers,

"What happened? What are you doing inside?" asked Atrai,

"Uncle, we came here to visit the hills but we are stuck with this fire and we need your help to find our friend lost somewhere in the middle of the hills, please help us!" pleasing Saagar,

"First let us get you out from this gate, wait," says Atrai,

Atrai conversing with his workers pointing out at the gate,

"First, we will get these boys out from here, I don't think we can turn down this tree upon the gate, let's get some people for help, once we enter inside we could walk up there," says Atrai pointing at the hills,

"Sir, what if you come inside so that we could bring our lost friend, please...!" said Saagar,

"Yea we will help! Don't worry" says Atrai,

"How come this big tree fell upon the gate?" asks Atrai,

"We don't know we just came hearing the huge sound!" says Cheyyar pointing at the middle of the hills,

"Okay, no problem, let's try to fix it!" says Atrai,

Atrai turned toward his colleagues,

“What's your plan,” asks Atrai,

Atrai observed the gate and the burning tree upon it, workers slightly turned towards the big wall that surrounded the bottom of the hill,

“We have some spare clothes which we can drop towards the other end of the wall so that the boys can hold it and we can pull from our end then boys will climb easily,” says worker,

“Ok! Let’s not waste the time, go get the tent cloths,” said Atrai,

Workers rushed towards the van,

“Why did you guys come alone here? Where are your parents?” asked Atrai,

“We came from the school directly, we couldn’t get our parents,” said Cheyyar,

“Kid... What you have done is wrong... which school are you guys from?” asks Atrai,

“Five Elements school!” says Saagar,

“Oh, the one which is conducting the event today, right?” asks Atrai,

“Yes, sir” responded Cheyyar,

“We are the organizers for your school today... Installing stages, lighting, and chairs” says Atrai,

"I know your teachers and principal very well, I will inform them about your irresponsibility!" says Atrai,

Workers brought the extended cloth! Atrai got the stone and tied it to the edge of the cloth and throws it to another side of the large wall, Saagar and Cheyyar step back, the first throw failed but the second throw took the life of the cloth with a weight of fortune that never broke, gradually dropped as a godsend destiny from the wall of soul,

"Boys remove the stone and tie it firmly to your hips and when we start to pull, you should try to walk on the wall balancing yourself properly" screams Atrai from the other end of the wall,

"Ok!" says Saagar,

"I will go first, please..." says Cheyyar and rushed towards the cloth removing the tied stone, and hurried to tie it on his hip,

Saagar kicked Cheyyar from the back and helped him to tie harder, workers on the other end started to hold the cloth appropriately tying to their hands and asked the boys,

"Shall we start!" asks Atrai,

"Yes!" shouted Cheyyar,

Atrai and workers started to pull the cloth slowly, and the cloth started to chafe on the edge of the sharp stone at the wall and Atrai found the cloths getting damaged, workers turned to Atrai,

"Boss?" asks worker,

"We don't have any choices... continue!" says Atrai,

Suddenly Cheyyar's leg slipped while walking on the wall and gets a slight hit, workers do feel the pressure, Saagar jumps and holds his leg and pushes upward and Cheyyar managed to steady himself on the wall,

"Boy, walk slowly...! Bend yourself and tighten the legs towards the wall, concentrate on your step towards the proper grip" shouts Atrai,

Cheyyar struggled to balance himself but somehow managed to pick his healthy figure and made it to the top,

"Boss, it's time for the boy to jump!" said Workers,

"Whoops..." says Atrai, and turned upwards,

"Now, jump...!" says Atrai to Cheyyar,

Scared Cheyyar Inhaled deeply,

"We don't have all day! Jump...! Soon..." shouts Saagar from the bottom,

Sweating Cheyyar seemed afraid looking at the deep down with a few sighing him to jump,

"Don't worry kid, I am a good catcher" says Atrai smiling at Cheyyar,

Cheyyar closed his eye... screamed... then jumps off...! Atrai and Workers positioned rigidly and waited for the chubby boy Cheyyar to catch, Van driver Atrai and Workers got him like a wing floating in the air, Atrai drops Cheyyar and removes the knot from his hip and bought another stone and tied it to the edge of the cloth and throws it another end, the magical cloth of life savior drops slowly towards Saagar and he began to tie them on his hip and takes the positing near the wall, by then he heard someone running faster, and he turned towards his right then he found an old man rushing towards the gate from the small passage that caught up with full of fire and he jumps out of it whipping the fire on his old retro T-shirt,

“Somebody, please help us...” shouts old man,

Atrai and Workers were about to begin to pull Saagar out of the chaos but they paused for a moment, Atrai leaves the hold of the magic cloth and walks to the gate bending his head and looking at the burning tree above him,

“A couple burnt themselves accidentally, they left unconscious in front of my house, they are fighting for their lives, it seems like they are on their last moment of breath... please save them, need your help!” says old man,

“Oh my god, how many?” asks Atrai,

“Some of them ran away from here when this wrath started,” says old man,

Old man looks right and left,

“Even the Jeep drivers seem to be disappeared,” said old man,

“Saagar... wait for some time,” says Atrai,

“Tell me, how can we get inside?” asks Atrai to the old man,

“Exact one kilometer backward from this highway, there is a small gap between these huge walls to enter the forest, I will wait for you over there... please make it fast!” said old man,

Atrai runs on the highway road and workers told,

“Hey boy, stick in front of this gate and look after your friend and also keep an eye on the vehicle at the main road,” says Worker and ran with their boss,

Atrai walks faster on the highway, he turned back and found his workers following him,

“If you find the old man, let me know guys!” said Atrai,

Atrai and Workers strode looking at the slopes sideways, the dark place under the slant covered with a lot of trees and plants, Atrai couldn’t find the old man, he kept turning his head and eye faster,

“Boss... old man is down here!” says Workers,

Atrai returned and glance at the slope sideways searching for old man,

“Where is he?” asks Atrai,

The place was covered with a lot of plants and trees, workers helped him to find the old man, and the team started to crawl slowly in the slant holding tiny stones for grip, and got down towards the hill border and entered the lower part of the forest where the old man stood,

“Follow me,” says old man,

Few spots on the slope have caught up with fire and the old man told,

“This place is also, lit too...” asks Atrai,

“Let us help the couple first and then I will return here with water to fix it,” says old man,

Atrai and his team continued to follow the old man, while everyone could hear the scream of the burnt couple, old man starts to walk faster, and the Atrai started to run and as they get closer to the house, they could notice two persons blacked out with red peeling skin lying down in front of the house, the painful scream flowing in the air to everyone ears beyond the running legs it is a soul that becomes tired yet the sympathy push them towards the strugglers, as soon as they reach with an uncontrollable breathe they found the couples cloth and skin were burnt and injured very badly and kept wobbling with a scream due to the pain,

"Injuries seem to be heavy," says Workers,

Atrai rushed inside the old man's house and gets a huge cloth and covered both of them,

"From how many hours are they struggling here?" asks Atrai to old man,

"Forty-Five minutes!" says old man,

"Forty-Five minutes? Seriously...? What were you doing all this time" asks Atrai,

"When I saw this couple out of my house... They were burning like anything, due to which they were not able to stand in one place, and I tried running behind with water to pour on them efficiently but it took time!" says old man,

"Gosh!" murmurs Atrai,

"I am helpless to take the decisions, hence I came near the gate seeking for some help, by then a god like you! Turned up here!" says old man,

Worried Atrai looks at the couple,

"What shall we do now? Are there any hospitals nearby?" asks Atrai,

"We have one in the town, it is around twenty-kilometer from here," says old man,

Atrai looks at the small path which is completely burning and asks the old man,

"Where does this path lead to?" asks Atrai,

"To the main gate," says old man,

"Oh, is it? Then how did you manage to reach the gate with so much fire in this path?" asks Atrai with his enlarged eye,

"We are used to it," says old man,

"Can we lift this couple in this path to my vehicle? asks Atrai,

"The path is completely burning, I made it but nobody can, it's too risky...!" says old man,

"Lifting both from the slope to the highway is harder," said Atrai,

Everybody looked at each other's faces,

"Boss... We will manage to lift" says workers,

Atrai turned here and there with a tensed face,

"It is not that easy my boys, you saw that slope, right?" asks Atrai,

“It took quite a time for us to get down, how do we climb without a grip? That too lifting them carefully?” said Atrai,

“And we should reach early to the vehicle so that we can get to the hospital as faster as we can,” said Atrai,

“Don’t worry boss, we can do this!” said workers,

Atrai turned towards the worker, they seemed pretty confident,

“Boss, we are already late, trust me we can do it,” says workers,

“Yes, we don’t have any choice! We should leave immediately or the couple might leave us, it’s now or never!” says old man,

“Okay let’s start, Lift them along with the cloth,” says Atrai to workers,

“No, wait... The cloths might tear apart” says old man, and went inside the house,

Later he comes out with some heavy bamboo pipes on his shoulder and a few green roots in his hand, which workers took from him and dropped on the ground, they arranged all the bamboo in a row and starts tying them with green roots,

“Tie properly!” says Atrai,

Old man and Atrai lifted the couple to set them on the combined bamboo, later Atrai joins worker to tie the bamboo faster,

“Come on... Faster!” says Atrai,

Atrai, two workers, and old man stood at four corners holding the edge of bamboo and lifted, old man and Atrai stood towards the front then the workers kept back and started to move slowly towards the slope of the highway,

Saagar from inside the gate,

“Hey dude, can you try to pull the cloth,” asks Saagar,

“Dude, let’s wait for the Van driver to return,” says Cheyyar and turned towards the empty highway expecting their arrival,

“Where are these uncles?” murmurs Saagar,

“Buddy, how did we miss Bhadra, I am still confused about it,” asks Cheyyar,

The burning tree up on the gate gets a mild shake and grabs the attention of boys, scared Cheyyar and Saagar stepped back and slowly looked at it,

Burnt ashes that faded in the air, bearing determination of a heaven's gate, lives that bonded within the burning woods, the unexpected destiny of a dying bird, unfortunate clouds that emerged vast, hearts that beating faster to the speechless children, eyes that filled with the shredding faith,

Atrai and his team put a lot of energy to carry the couple, meanwhile, some trees are blocking their way but they planned to move zig-zag to control the blocks, old man and Atrai also found that some paths were caught up with fire, at very early they kept themselves aside looking at the tree block and turned to avoid the danger,

Cheyyar kept looking at the highway and expecting Atrai to return as soon as possible for rescue, suddenly a white flash blinds them for a while and slowly the flash fades to normal, the boys were speechless for a while, and slowly looked up at the sky, it is a huge thunder again swarming in the cloud above the hill,

Team that holding the couple, heard the sound of thunder... that rhythms continuously at the flying hills, and the couple mildly started to shiver,

"Keep moving," says the Atrai,

As the magnanimous thunder moved in the clouds and also few lives kept moving in the forest, Atrai and his team reached the slope and set down the bamboo holder to the ground, relaxing four pillars while he looks at the huge slope and kept gazing at it!

The old man looks at everyone and picks up the root tied at one side of the bamboo and climbs the slope, went upwards and tied to a tree on the highway, and crawled backward on the slope,

"We don't have enough time! Pick up the root and let's tie to the tree up there" says old man,

"Then?" asks Atrai,

"Then, we will pull the root so that the bamboo streams upward in the slope," says old man,

Atrai looks at the couple struggling with the pain, immediately everyone picks up the left-over roots at the edges and went upwards to the highway and tied it to a tree,

"My self and old man will pull upwards, you both go down and hold the couples to stick with the bamboo!" says Atrai to his workers,

Workers got down at slope rapidly even after it was hurting them,

"Try to push from the backside if possible but careful!" said Atrai to the workers,

Old man and Atrai started to the pull the roots slowly and the sleeping couples kept moving along with bamboo and a small stone on the slope hitting bamboo and the brilliant workers kept lifting the bamboo whenever the bamboo got held by the stone from moving, the maximum strength drains out Atrai and old man, workers started to push from behind to keep progressing, kept pushing and pushing...

Bamboo that reached almost the upper part of the slope by then, the tired old man lost hold on the root and the bamboo starts going backward on the slope, workers putting more effort into pushing upwards, Atrai tries to hold stiff from the bamboo moving backward, couple lying towards the edge of the bamboo on rolling down, struggling couple shouts and old man gets cautious with lot of sweat on his face then wipes it and took a long breath and holds the upper side of bamboo that is almost reached,

"Keep your legs on the small stones near you," says Atrai to his employees at the slope,

Pressurized hands of Atrai holding the roots that are exhausting and slowly his fingers were slipping the root from his control,

"Sir please hold we are almost done," says Worker,

Old man struggles to pull one corner of the bamboo and Atrai's energy ended due to which root slipped from his hand, employees kept the steady hold from the back but one side of top was gripped by old man yet trying to hold steady but it made the bamboo to turn around and crawl downwards which led to wobble and the couples started to scream for the heavy pain...

There comes a lion heart Cheyyar, ran towards the root that is rapidly going down and he grabs it, old man with his struggling voice asks Cheyyar,

“What.... are... you... doing... here...” asks old man,

“I just came searching for all of you,” says Cheyyar holding the rope rigidly,

Atrai relaxed for a second and joins them to pull the bamboo upward, later on, they lifted couple to the highway,

“Wait, I will get my vehicle here,” says Atrai and runs back to the main gate,

Cheyyar looked at the couple who were burnt very badly, he gets scared looking at their scorched faces,

Saagar looked at Atrai and ran towards the vehicle also Atrai looks at Saagar and walked towards him by then Saagar prepared to tie the cloth on his hip and stood near the wall to climb,

“Boy, come here...! You have to listen to me carefully, one couple is struggling for their life, it is very crucial, we need to get them to the hospital immediately, I will inform the old man to come here and rescue you and your friend who is stuck up there!” said Atrai and walks back to the vehicle and makes an immediate U-turn towards the couple at the highway,

Cheyyar looks at the burnt couple and looks at a person with a red dress which seems fishy, kind of similar to a couple wearing while standing at the bottom when they were all together at the mid part of the hills throwing the stone at them, burnt lady screaming for help, Cheyyar with the tear bends his head and his heart starts to feel an essence of sadness and guilt, he looks at the old man who also seems to be having the tear in his eye,

"Calm down... my dear children," says old man to the burnt couple, workers wiping their tears and kept removing the tied root in the bamboo,

Highly burning sound that accompanies the lonely Saagar standing near the gate, he turns back to the road near the flex board expecting Bhadra to return, but it seems unfortunate,

Atrai rushed in the vehicle to spot where the couples are lying and told his worker,

"Make some space at the trailer, let them rest behind," says Atrai,

"Who knows the exact location of the hospital?" asks Atrai,

Old man and Cheyyar looked at the Atrai,

"I know," says Cheyyar at the same time,

Atrai looked at both and spoke to old man,

"Let's do one thing, old man please go to the gate and help Saagar and his friend who is stuck somewhere in the hills, I will take Cheyyar along with me, he will guide me to the hospital," says Atrai,

"Come with me!" said Atrai to Cheyyar and walks towards the vehicle,

Old man and workers lift the couple carefully and dropped them behind the vehicle trailer, Atrai at the front seat starts the vehicle old man walks to the front wiping his sweat,

“Try to reach as early as possible, they are struggling a lot!” says old man to Atrai,

Cheyyar sat next to Atrai and turned toward the old man to the window next to Atrai,

“Please look after my friend Saagar and Bhadra, please,” says Cheyyar,

“Yes, Child I will... guide him to the proper location,” says old man,

“How can this old man manage everything all alone,” asks old man,

“You are not old, we are, I saw your strength all this time sir, Keep going!” says Atrai,

“There are few other villagers who might be stuck inside the hills, and don’t know what happened to the unspeakable lives up there, whom do I save?” asks old man,

“Please try to manage sir and you are very good at it...” says Atrai,

“If possible, get the help of boy near the gate... please do something,” says Atrai,

“As soon as I reach the hospital, I will immediately send the crowds to help you here,” said Atrai and left the spot,

Old man got down in the slope and ran towards the main gate, Saagar stood in front of the gate expecting anybody’s presence for his help, old man walks with a slight burn on his legs and arms in the path that has completely caught up with fire,

“How did your friend get out?” asks old man,

"Atrai and his worker pulled him through this cloth," says Saagar and shows the cloth to old man,

"Ok!" says old man,

Suddenly a different type of scream from the hills, old man looks back towards the hilltop,

"Seems to be animals," says old man,

Some spots in the hills have started to burn, old man left in shock looking at the fire in some parts of the flying hill,

Slowly he keeps his head down to normal, and found a big stone at the side of the path, he went closer to it and picks the stone putting a lot of energy,

"Get back!" shouts old man to Saagar,

Suddenly he screamed with the painful strength and ran towards the gate and throws the stone upon the gate... stone bangs into the gate... burning tree stuck upon it, slowly rotates and the branches stacked to the sharp edges of the gate and stopped from falling, old man and Saagar expecting the tree to fall, the burning tree kept slipping down from the gate at tortoise speed, old man slowly walks near the gate looking at the tree above him and picks the stone and walks back, again he ran shaking his body completely to the left to right and throws it to the gate, and run backward immediately and Saagar looks at him and ran backward too, huge burning tree rapidly fell from the gate making the huge sound, the burning branches broke and spreads all around it and the small fire particles flying for the force of tree bashing to the ground,

The broken tree reduced its fire, by splitting its fire around the gate, Saagar walks out of the main gate from the small gap between the tree and gate, old man tries to turn off the fire from tiny branches that spilled out of the tree, Saagar walks out and stood in front of the main gate and looked at the hilltop and it reminds him of a few hours ago when they got down from the bus, the calm and beautiful flying hills which now seems like an inferno,

"Grandpa... one of my friends is stuck above there! Please help me to find him" says Saagar,

"You both came together, and how you missed one?" asked old man,

"He looks tiny and who doesn't speak, we were in a hurry to hide from the thunder, but we missed him while running faster," says Saagar,

"We have big things to do, child..." says old man,

"Please help me, I took him here without anybody's permission, if I don't take him back, I will be rusticated from the school," says Saagar,

Old man looked at Saagar,

"You should start obeying the elders first..." murmurs old man,

Saagar with his helpless and afraid look stood silent,

"Come let's find him," says old man,

Both started to walk towards the flying hills, unfortunately, the chaos that has started to shock the old man,

"What is this?" old man asks himself,

Looking at the roads that are blocked by the small burning trees all around the hills,

Bhadra rolled inside a deep slope for a while and woke up wiping dust in his arms and visualized a transformed green into a red mist and the flame reflection in his eye kept moving along with burnt trees, he could feel the shadows that are running around faster, a giant stomps that moving rapidly inside the dust, he sat aside closing his eye with two hands for few minutes,

Old man and Saagar kept moving observing the tiny smoke at different locations on the hill, Saagar feels afraid for Bhadra's situation, and the old man is afraid of others living in the forest,

Once again, a very strong thunder hits the forest, scared Bhadra again covered his eye, animals that were running gets panic and sprinted more faster, a tiger roars and Bhadra opened his eye it jumps above him like a star falling in the sky, the trumpet of an elephant leads Bhadra to hide again, swift of a rapid lion expressed the unease to all the living things with a howl while Bhadra started to shiver, an ostrich's fast legs sprinting towards the sagacious destiny Bhadra opens his half eye and looks at all the animals spreading inside the forest to the unknown paths, some feathers that caught up with fire and some saving itself from the end of life, some screaming in the pain and some wail for the help, a black panther with shedding tears walks slowly towards Bhadra, scared Bhadra moves aside but the depressed panther bows in front of him and sat next to him, meanwhile a long python caught with fire moves behind rapidly, Bhadra gets scared looking at the python and gets closer to the panther, until the prolonged python kept moving aside for few minutes, fire particles that flying in front of his eye reminds him of the stone that was thrown by Cheyyar to the couples few hours ago that went and hit their fire woods and spilled with fire particles, once again the thunder strike brings Bhadra back to present which makes him to see the black panther clearly and its emerald green eye reflects the burning trees falling apart gradually, dishearten panther looked at Bhadra and also he looks at it with a mild tear from his eye, a language both shared with each other was less but a powerful tear had its own meaningful voice.

RISE OF A MINIATURE

Every photo frame preserves its memory, moments that capture the feeling of presence but not the future of unknown, some frame that holds the memory of a smile by Krishna and Yamuna together, some frames that speak the experience of their family vacation, Krishna on the bed kept looking at a photo in his room, his wife smiling and her beautiful eye reminds him of both holding their hand and walking together besides flying hill,

"What is your uttermost wish, dear?" asks Krishna,

"Like every woman on this planet, I too have a dream of having a good family which is already happened to me..."

"How about you?" asked Yamuna,

Krishna looks into her eye,

"I always had a wish to see the beauty of this world along with a wonderful family of mine!" said Krishna

"Yes... me too..." said Yamuna with a beautiful smile,

Krishna again turned to her looked at her eyes and stepped forward slowly holding her hands,

"My wish is always to take care of my cute babies," said Krishna and kept staring at her eye,

Out of the same eye from the photo, Krishna comes back to the present lying on the bed, impounding the breath of love that shatters the desired intimacy, a guilt that is spreading in the veins, and forgiveness that unbinds with the destiny, Krishna got up, walked closer to the photo and looked at her eye, then slowly turns back and walked out of the house, took his motorcycle and started to search Yamuna to apologize as he felt, his eyes are desperately looking for his love in the sky where stars do breathe, and his love that found standing at the bus stand, Krishna stopped his bike looking at Yamuna,

“Don’t know what mindless thing he is going to do now!” says Netravati looking at Krishna,

Yamuna looked at him getting down from his bike and Krishna walks closer to them while many leaves from the tree slowly kept falling for the unexpected wind approach the village after a very long time, Netravati looked at the trees waving slowly for the wind and feels very dramatic,

“Netravati... I’m sorry...” says Krishna,

Women's left speechless,

“Trying to impress your wife now, huh? All this time where was your mind?” asks Netravati,

Yamuna slightly smiled and Krishna says,

“You need to know one thing, due to work pressure I do have a lot of tensions, all I want is to spend time with my family but she seems to be busy all the time with reasons, which leads me to get angry, even I am human right, I do get angry and other emotions,” said Krishna,

A mystical wagon with wings, came flying to spread one of the elements, some destined in it to the heavens and some in the fortune that wait at future and for some to their houses like another normal day, Sailing voyage that could change one's fortune but not for the forgotten souls... they had their potion of luck in the pockets, it's been said that one's decision is in a favor of unconnected experience when it seemed alright to the world, the bus was alive only when it had wheels in it, a destiny that loved to rotate with a breathing wanderer until the existence of love,

The bus came...! Netravati and Yamuna stepped ahead towards the bus to board,

"Netravati...!" shouts Krishna,

Both turns towards Krishna and also people inside the bus never minded but few did,

"You board the bus... we both will come in the bike," told Krishna to Netravati,

Netravati looked at Yamuna then she smiled,

"If he troubles you again, remember you should leave him...!" says Netravati to Yamuna and got onto the bus,

The mystical wagon with the wings flew, meanwhile Krishna left his bike aside and walks to Yamuna,

"Yamu... I'm sorry...!" says Krishna,

"You do mistakes and later you agree to it," asks Yamuna,

Krishna kept silent...

"Precautions are always prevention... why don't you understand? Try to control yourself before you start exploding" says Yamuna,

"I asked you sorry... And I mean it dear..." says Krishna,

"It's not your mess... It's the firewater inside you... these negative shades will end when you quit consuming it" says Yamuna,

"When are you going to accept that even you too were part of all these messes..." asks Krishna,

The smile that was about to fade while a cold wind that outbreaks from the macrocosm, both started to shiver... Yamuna looks up at the sky, a very big cloud that slowly crawling like a god of clouds that walked here as he was missing us all,

"Something is wrong," says Yamuna and looked at her watch for the time,

"What?" asks Krishna and he turns upward,

"I have never seen such a dark could in our town," says Yamuna,

"Yeah, never in my life," said Krishna and removes his sweater and gave it to Yamuna,

"I believe, another one-week winter should start dear..." said Krishna,

"Then it should be the first rain in the village," asks Yamuna,

"Yes," replied Krishna,

"It's going to be an unstoppable rain, I think we should being our son to the house as early as possible before the rain starts," said Yamuna,

Even after wearing the sweater, Yamuna kept shivering,

"So much cold?" asks Krishna and turns around...

An old man collating woods to burn them,

"Come let's go there..." says Krishna and took Yamuna,

Old man looked at both walking towards the coppice, with a smile he welcomed both, he noticed Yamuna was shivering a lot, immediately he sets on the fire,

"Where are you both from?" ask old man,

"We do stay a kilometer away from here!" said Krishna,

"One kilometer? I have never seen you both" asks old man,

"I leave my house too early in the morning to my work and return late at night also... We do come out of the house once in a while" says Krishna,

"That's why!" said old man,

Yamuna and Krishna stood in front of the firewood and stretched their hands and rubbed slowly to warm themselves up, the old man gets a few more planks of wood to keep the fire consistent,

"Thank you so much!" said Krishna,

"My pleasure," says old man,

“Let me help you!” says Krishna and thought of picking some woods from him,

“I’m too young to manage it, kid, don’t worry,” says old man,

“A man like you will always be a role model for us Sir...” said Krishna,

“It’s my responsibility for years...” says old man,

“You are doing this for years?” asks Krishna,

“You are impressing us,” said Krishna,

Yamuna and Krishna looked at old man and feel happy,

“Sorry to bother you again, but can you get us some water to drink,” asks Krishna,

“My house is a bit far from here... can you wait until I return?” asks old man

“It’s ok, please don’t strain yourself...” says Yamuna,

“It's rather a gratification,” says old man and walks to his house,

Hemavati with her friends in the queue excited to get inside the scary house, mob behind them pushing, Hemavati be the first one in the queue trying to control from falling, meanwhile, teacher Manimala arrived in front of the queue and started to collect tickets, gradually the students in the queue started to make noises,

“Silence,” says Manimala and starts collecting the ticket,

“Do not rush...” shouts Manimala,

Hemavati with her friends including Tapi and a few other batch students behind them entered the scary house, Manimala stops the queue,

“Mam... I’m with them...” said Ashoka,

“Wait until they return, only ten members are allowed per batch,” says Manimala and stops Ashoka for the next turn,

Excited students in the queue started to make noise, while Hemavati and other students stood at the entrance of the scary house looking at the dark on the inside, as soon as they entered the door closed hardly and the girl from the gang got scared and screamed for it, Hemavati and some students do laugh,

“It's just the door,” says Hemavati and continues to laugh,

Students outside, heard the girls screaming from the inside and everybody maximized their eyes and started murmuring,

“Maintain the silence,” says Manimala,

All the boys behind Hemavati and the gang started to scare the girls by shouting and making different noises at the entrance, the girl who is already scared and starts sweating heavily, Hemavati touches her shoulder to calm her down but again she shouts,

“Hey, Narmada... Don’t get scared... it's your class leader here” said Hemavati,

A voice from a speaker inside the scary house,

“Keep moving,” said Organizers,

Some students in the unknown paths of dark kept walking, Tapi tried to look around with a minimal red light inside and kept following some shadows passing near to him

"Hemavati? Is that you...?" asks Tapi,

No one responded... After a few seconds, Tapi inhales and exhales faster, his legs started to shiver slightly, other students in the silence gulp down and sweats, the boys behind Hemavati and the gang shouted at them to move faster, and the girls got scared then started to push themselves and Hemavati searched for Tapi, but he kept moving ahead silently, some of the spots inside the scary house has the lights at the floor, girls started to walks faster looking here and there, Tapi stops... A dead-end! No route further... he kept closer to the wall and slowly a light from the top fades in... a wall in front of him, he turns to the right and its empty then turned to the left shocked looking at a scary zombie face with a horror mouth, Tapi kept looking at it continuously and steps back, suddenly the eyes of it started rotating upwards and down, Tapi starts to scream, rotating eye opens the door from the wall at the center and he runs into it and found a light path inside the second stage, a speaker from somewhere said,

"Keep moving...!"

The lights in the path slowly turns on and turns off continuously, Tapi found a face rotating and laughing constantly, Tapi kept running in the light path, Hemavati and her gang kept walking slowly one girl from her gang told,

"Hey look at this light, I believe it should be the path and we can follow them!"

Hemavati and her friends felt right and started to follow the path of the light,

"Where did this Tapi go..." says Hemavati,

"Who knows, he should have got scared and rushed early to the exit!" says a girl from the gang,

Girls kept laughing and moved further, other batch students behind the girls murmuring about the upcoming hurdles they are about-face, an empty steel cage in front of Tapi with a red light inside, suddenly a big devil ran from left to right and came towards Tapi... it rushes shouting at him and hits the cage and started to pull the cage very harder and screaming,

"Open the cage...!"

Tapi fell off to the ground, then slowly moved his head towards the cage, the face of the devil inside it was very cruel, Tapi got up slowly looking at it and runs away, girls walking with the light path and reached a wall where there is no way, slowly the light fades in and another girl from Hemavati gang turns right and saw the zombie face on the wall and runs backward hitting all the students, then Hemavati saw the zombie face rotating its eye and she steps back slowly,

"It's just a three-dimensional mask, designed in plastic don't get scared," said Hemavati,

The door slowly opens to the second stage and all the girls rushed in, Tapi enters a path where skeletons are hanging Tapi bends himself and started to run but some legs of the skeletons kept knocking on his head, girls found the empty cage and kept passing ahead, suddenly a devil ran inside the cage from left to right and towards the students shouting... girls started to run away from the cage following the light path, other batch students behind the girls found the screaming devil inside the cage and started to laugh at it,

"Go away, idiot!"

All the boys from different batch started to laugh at the crazy devil inside the cage, well-acted devil inside the cage stops screaming and steps back to the room inside the cage, girls walking fast and kept covering their ears for the horrible screaming sounds, light path that leads Tapi to another closed wall with a colored rope from the top and thought of climbing the rope but it wasn't reachable to him, a small baby behind him called, Tapi turned back... a medium size doll smiling at him with pink hairs, red lipsticks and a stripe tee, Tapi staring at the plastic doll continuously and there is no action from it but hushed at the spot with no movement, it's a continuous stare that slightly doubtful but Tapi tries to move on to his left and suddenly the doll's eye looked at his leg and rotates back to him with a still smiling face, Tapi's heart beating faster looking its eye movement, doll suddenly opens knife and screams, scared Tapi gets frustrated, the doll starts to run towards him, Tapi had no way behind him, he taps the wall behind him while the doll running towards him, slowly the wall opened and he shifted to other stage and landed to a room that has small light, suddenly a wooden ground that opens a bottom stage of a mob of zombies tied to a pole and release themselves and heading towards Tapi, he started to scream and also the devils were, Kept looking here and there for the doors but it seems like this stage had no doors, zombies are nearing and Tapi started to shiver, got up and tried to run all the possible way to hit the walls to find the exit by then the devils started to run faster towards him, Tapi closed his eye and covered his ear from both the hands, few minutes later he felt something is moving, his body kept hovering like someone is carrying him, slowly he opened one of his eye, and found himself on a chair which also had wheels on it, the chair slowly kept moving on a track, a roller coaster like chair moves up and down and gradually increased the speed, while the chair moving a few devils stood aside screaming at him, and he found a cage where zombies chasing small children inside it, yet the chair kept moving fast towards the end and stood near a tall zombie stunned without moving, Tapi got down looking at it and slowly walks away from it, the tall zombie kept looking at him passing but there were no actions, then Tapi enters a room and found a door seemed like an exit, he entered and walks faster towards the door by then a devil similar to his length walks to him and told

"I'm you, died yesterday in flying hills..." Ghost Tapi,

Tapi smiled... then,

"I will give you a lot of chocolates, stay with me!" says Ghost Tapi with a smile,

Tapi pushed the ghost aside and passed over it, Tapi walked to the door and prayed.

"God, I'm not capable to face another stage, let this be the end!" murmurs Tapi,

And pushes the door and finally, the brightness of the sun strikes his mind and soul-soothing him, the fresh air brings peace then he took a long breath and wiped his sweat and opened his eye slowly,

"What the evil" murmurs Tapi,

Turned back towards the exit door,

"Heaven's gate!" murmurs Tapi,

Slowly walked out with the satisfaction of being pleasant,

"Tapi...!" shouts Ashoka,

Tapi looked at the queue in front of the scary house, Ashoka and other students behind him pushing to the front and pulling back, Manimala trying to control the mob's force by yelling at them, Tapi walked towards him with a strange expression on his face, excited Ashoka asks,

“Hey... how was it?” asks Ashoka,

“Very much thrilled,” says Tapi,

Students in the queue heard about Tapi's experience and feels more excited,

“Is it a worthful experience?” asks Ashoka,

“Yes, they have nailed it, much better compared to last year, I got pissed off dude...” says Tapi,

Ashoka enthused and laughs,

“All those zombies inside are our seniors on the makeup,” said Ashoka,

“Is it?” asks Tapi,

“Yes, you should have ragged them,” said Ashoka,

“Imagine what happened to the girls, let’s wait for their reaction,” said Ashoka,

“Yeah, I never saw them after entering inside!” said Tapi,

“I am damn sure they will come out crying,” said Ashoka,

Hemavati came out bending her head and slowly crawling like a butterfly,

“Tapi, they are out,” said Ashoka pointing towards the exit of the scary house,

Hemavati walked out with tears and Ashoka in the queue looked at her and keeps laughing, also other students in the queue started to make noises, but with no response, she kept walking with tears, and her friends with the other batch of students walks out behind one by one with a great experience apart from Hemavati, Manimala at the entrance starts letting few more students inside the scary house,

“Dude, once I am out, let’s try to search Bhadra, wait here...!” said Ashoka and enters the scary house,

“Ok,” said Tapi and kept looking at Hemavati passing away with tears,

A friend of hers came to Tapi,

“Where were you?” asks Narmada,

“I was lost in the dark,” said Tapi,

“Why didn't you stick with us,” asks Narmada,

“I told you it was dark?” replied Tapi,

“Then how we did stick together,” asks Narmada,

“What happened?” asks Tapi and turned strangely towards Hemavati passing far away towards the classroom,

Narmada kept scolding him continuously,

“Until and unless you don’t let me know... I can't respond anything!” says Tapi,

“Other batch students, who were behind us, have misbehaved with Hemavati inside the scary house, and we were searching for you to seek help but you weren't there!” said Narmada,

“Oh gosh!”

Tapi gets tensed and speechless for a minute,

“You should have slapped those insects!” shouts Tapi,

“Dude, what's the point?” asks Narmada,

“At least you should have dragged them towards the Teacher Manimala, right?” asked Tapi,

“Dude, they are punished don’t worry, but you weren't there with us! And that’s the problem” said Narmada,

“I did not get you?” questioned Tapi,

Narmada told the flashback to Tapi about the incident,

“At a point when Hemavati screamed, our luck stood by us, the zombies inside with the makeup were our seniors who heard Hemavati's voice and came for our help,” says Narmada,

“Oh” murmurs Tapi,

“When another batch of students came behind us teasing, our seniors removed the mask and brought the lights into the darkness and warned them seriously,” says Narmada,

“Why did you misbehave with this girl?” asks Senior,

Boys kept silent,

“Come let’s go to the principal, I will make sure all of you are rusticated from the school immediately,” says Senior,

“We aren't sure what happened? We were behind these girls and had maintained a distance from the beginning” said boys,

Senior kept staring seriously at them,

“We promise, we haven't done anything,” says other batch boys,

“If not you! Who did it?” shouts Senior,

Boys quiver,

“We don’t know, I was leading our team in the front and our boys were behind me, nobody stepped ahead to misbehave with these girls and I can promise that I haven't done anything!” says other section boys,

“Don’t lie to me...!” senior shouted once again very strongly,

All the students next to him got scared,

“We aren't interested in torturing these girls, please leave us,” said other section boys,

Senior asked Hemavati,

“Did you see this guy coming to you?” asks senior,

Crying Hemavati replied,

"No...!"

"Okay fine, girls you take her to the principal and complain about the incident and inform the presence of whoever entered in the first batch," said Senior,

Narmada completes with the flashback, saddened Tapi stood speechless and she left with a disappointment, a few minutes later Ashoka walks out of the scary house laughing very loud, Tapi turned and Ashoka walks to Tapi,

"Hey, sorry I made you wait... What happened? Your eyes seem to be wet!" asks Ashoka,

Tapi told him about the incident inside the scary house, but Ashoka kept silent,

"Where are those girls now?" asks Ashoka,

"They might have gone to the principal's office to complain!" says Tapi,

"Even, you will be called, I believe," said Ashoka,

"Dude, why me? What's my fault?" asks Tapi,

"You entered together, right?" asks Ashoka,

"I was unable to see anything, and it was too scary in there, I ran out as fast as possible, how is that going to be my fault?" asks Tapi,

"Because you entered with them," said Ashoka,

Tapi gets angry,

"I will inform the principal that I wasn't there in that situation" replies Tapi,

"Leave that, let's try to find your cousin first!" said Ashoka,

"No man, they haven't turned up yet I believe, I have a skit to perform, don't know how I will concentrate with so many issues that are rushing towards us," says worried Tapi,

"Let's do one thing, I will search for Bhadra and Saagar and one more...?" murmurs Ashoka,

"Cheyyar!" says Tapi,

"Yeah, right... Cheyyar, I will help you find them, you try to prepare for the skit" said Ashoka,

"Dude that's not the problem...!" says Tapi,

"Then what?" asks Ashoka,

"The main character in our skit is Hemavati, and now it seems like she won't turn up to perform," says Tapi,

"Oh yes, that's the problem right!" said Ashoka,

"For the first time, I am performing on a stage! I feel that my dream is getting vanished at a very close call dude!" says Tapi,

"Dude, don't worry! Everything is going to be alright, now let's not waste time on chatting, we will try to convince her" said Ashoka,

Demoralized Tapi lifts his head and looks into Ashoka's eye,

“You are right... at least we will try” says Tapi,

Fire god summoned to dedicate his energy, uninvited thunder piercing into the flying hills, a wind of luck trying to rescue unspeakable lives in burning forest, every next is an immense dream while humans thrive to save themselves, breathing in between fire and thunder gods dark cloud, where the time runs slower to endure the ambiance but old man inside the time tries to walks faster looking at some spots in hills that covered with red mist, desperate eye looking around at every corner to find Bhadra,

“What’s the age of your friend?” asks old man,

“Four to five years,” said Saagar,

“You aren't aware of his age properly?” asks old man,

Saagar at silence,

“I met him today, he is my friend's cousin,” says Saagar,

“Where is your friend then?” asks old man,

“He was busy in participating some activities in the school event,” says Saagar,

“First of all, without his brother, you have brought him here and you lost him! You should have been more responsible!” scolds old man,

Old man looked at speechless Saagar, and turns his head suspecting at the sideways, gradually the clouds seem alike occupying the entire flying hill with a small thunder worm walking in that grey cloud seems to calm down, old man and Saagar kept looking at their surrounding for Bhadra,

"We should walk faster," says old man,

Saagar pushes himself to walk faster and kept breathing heavily, then the old man looked at a burning fallen tree road blocked, some of its branches are spreading the fire to another way of the forest, old man found animals crossing in the fear from a small passage of the slope in sideways broken by a force of tree hitting them around, old man and Saagar walks faster near the tree, as soon as they were closer towards the burning tree, they heard a unique voice from the broken passage,

"Saagar, go..." says old man,

Saagar ran towards the passage and looked at the slope, he found a small path that is flowing downwards, old man came near slope and sat down kept looking continuously in the passage, burning huge tree causing a lot of temperature to both but old man tries to handle the heat while Saagar got away from the passage for not able to handle the overheat emitting from the tree, A deer runs faster next to him, Saagar got scared... Suddenly Saagar turns and makes a way to it, and the deer runs faster and jumps above the old man and enters the passage spreading mud and stomping the burnt plants and skids downwards in the passage, Saagar turns to the opposite side of the high hills and expecting for more animals to rush form upside but none appeared to be, kept looking all around the hills and at the roadside and he found a stall that is burning, suddenly it reminds him that it was the mid part of the hills where they stopped a few hours earlier to drink water, the place where they threw stones at the couples, spot when the thunder god appeared to be more expressive,

Saagar walks to old man,

"Sir!" says Saagar,

Old man did not respond,

"Sir...!" again says Saagar,

Old man looked at Saagar,

"We know this place, from here we missed him!" says Saagar,

Old man turns back to the deep-down passage analyzing for any activities,

"But there is no activity down there," says old man,

Old man pauses for a moment,

"It's impossible for him to be alive or to survive down there," says old man looking at the burning slope,

Old man's response made Saagar heartbreaking,

"Please do something," says Saagar,

Old man kept quiet,

"This is the place where we started to run and we missed him right over here," says Saagar,

Old man Inhales strongly and told

"Wait here...!" says old man to Saagar and then he jumps into the passage,

As soon as he jumped, he couldn't find any grip and started to float on a muddy slope, plant, and trees burning around keeps hitting his arms and leg, yet he keeps dodging as much as possible, and the slope gets more deeper-down and the old man starts to skid faster, burning trees and plant moving faster while the temperature is increasing, old man started to sweat, the burning sound that's weaving in his ear, old man in the speed drops at an empty spot and in the left with the same force he ran towards a black panther and fell upon it...

Resting injured black panther got troubled from the kick of old man, the old man got up and runs back from the black panther, panther looked at him with wet eye and slowly crawled back to its place and sat at the corner, old man understood that it is injured but not sure where and how old man turns around, a peacock with fire in its tail running around, a crying giraffe ran faster and fell, a scared elephant rushes stomping others in the ground,

"Why are you so merciless god?" murmurs old man,

Suddenly the panther in front of him got up and slowly walks towards him, then the old man got scared and kept looking at it moving but the panther walks beside him and sat next to Bhadra, old man found Bhadra sitting under an orange plant with a lot of fruits around him and he kept eating it, old man gets closer to Bhadra,

"Bhadra!" calls old man,

Bhadra got scared and threw the orange in his hand and turns back to the strange old man,

"Don't worry, I am Saagar's friend, came here to help you" says old man and picks him up,

Bhadra sat on his shoulder then old man looks at a few animals that are lying on the ground crying for its family,

“Situation has become worse than the hell!” murmurs old man,

Bhadra kept looking at the Black Panther lying,

“I have no control over this situation, we just have to leave this place without any aid for your friend,” says old man to Bhadra,

Bhadra did not respond anything, old man looks at the passage,

“It’s going to be hard to climb now,” says old man,

“Our grip is burnt to ash” murmurs old man,

Bhadra looking at the burning trees,

“The forest once green is now being turned to black metamorphosed by red god,” says old man and starts to climb,

Bhadra turns back to old man looking at him murmuring,

Saagar alone at the top murmurs,

“What if the old man returns without Bhadra?” murmurs Saagar,

He looks up at the sky,

“It's almost getting darker” again murmurs Saagar,

Saagar turned back immediately... hearing a sudden scream, deer came from the hilltop stuck into a metal side block in the road,

“Gosh” screams Saagar and ran closer to it,

The deer in search of its lost family, is unable to understand the cataclysm, unstoppable fear leading it to rush towards the unknown trap, Saagar jumps over the metal block and walks closer to the deer but it saw him coming and gets scared and gradually bows then also tries to pull back itself away from him but Saagar with all his energy tries lifting the metal block and pushes deer's leg from his feet, however, it keeps jumping back-to-back trying to pull its leg with too much of pressure out of the steel block that is causing severe injury to its feet, deer seemed to bear the injury and entail towards finding the family but with no option, it pulls out its feet with the little wound in its leg and moves jumping with three normal legs for few meters away from the burning tree and jumps into the side slope of the forest,

Old man bends, and slowly walks in the passage looking upward towards the hill road, a rapid hot wind is following in the passage traveling from all around the burning forest, old man tries to hold the burnt grey plant to pull himself up but it faded like a mist that flew in the air, Bhadra on the shoulder turned to his right and saw some animals caught with fire and some running upward struggling to push themselves up, some animals ran faster and got themselves hitting to a burning tree, old man slips with Bhadra on his shoulder he suddenly keeps his hand to the ground and holding Bhadra from another hand lifts himself back and keeps climbing the passage wiping his sweat, Saagar came back near the passage and saw old man with Bhadra on his shoulder struggling to climb,

"Do you want my help...!" shouts Saagar,

Old man looks at Saagar and kept climbing with no response, Saagar looks around to find something that could help them, however, the flying hill is left with only that is trending fire,

"Not sure, what situation my cousin is going through and it's my first skit today that is getting ruined," says Tapi,

“Don’t worry, difficulties won't last long... You just need patience...” says Ashoka,

“You don’t know about my uncle...”

“I mean Bhadra’s father... he is too aggressive... he bangs my aunt Yamuna for many things,” says Tapi,

“By the time the event starts, they might arrive... You should focus on preparing for the skit” says Ashoka,

Tapi with silence kept moving toward the classroom,

“Don’t you want the skit to be appreciated?” said Ashoka,

Speechless Tapi kept climbing the stairs inhaling the cold wind, and once they entered the classroom both found Hemavati in tears,

Old man stuck near the steep passage entry,

“Hey, help me...!” says old man,

Saagar bends himself stretching his hand, old man lifts Bhadra from his shoulder and passed on to Saagar, Saagar lifts Bhadra and brought him back to the road then old man holds on to a half-burnt tree next to him and pulled himself upward to the road, as soon as he came up... took a long breath and slowly walks to a stone aside and sat on it for a while,

“Are you tired?” asks Saagar to old man,

Old man looks up at the dark sky and gradually turned toward the burning hilltop, then slowly brings his eyes down to Saagar and Bhadra,

"Not me...! The forest is...!" said old man,

"Let's not waste time..." says old man,

All three start walking back to the main gate of flying hills while Saagar a foot behind both looked at wounded Bhadra with a mild happy tear in his eye on the return of the lost ones,

Burnt Birds screaming in the van, Cheyyar is unable to hear the painful scream, Atrai couldn't concentrate properly on driving yet he commits himself towards the hospital,

"Can someone try to calm them down, we are nearing the hospital in a few minutes" shouts Atrai to his workers who sat behind,

Cheyyar looks at the sky turning to dark pink and clouds gradually spreading the entire village,

"Hey boy, what are you looking at?" asks Atrai,

"Guide me properly, don't get distracted!" says Atrai,

"We are on right track," says Cheyyar and kept looking at passing zigzag roads,

Red dust in the forest exhibiting as an accessory escorted by wind, unrolling towards an adoring green for a moment the green sacrificed itself for temporary existence of blaze, as a last resort it believed that the lit never burnt by a love that voided in the peace of inner soul for which it was left unburnt and once in a while mighty blaze do appear to relinquish to overcome the paths of darkness and shine the hearts of spell caster,

"Lord, please help us...! Shower your tears for us and try to calm down our red guest who entered our hills" shouts old man and keeps moving,

Saagar holds Bhadra's hand firmly with an attentive movement, Bhadra's eye overflowing with the illustration of a black panther...! Unemotional emerald green eye, the unforgettable struggle of a black cat, old man rubs panther's head and understands that it could not choose to survive...!

"If you could walk with me till the entrance gate, I can get you some water and medicines," says old man to the panther rubbing its head,

Bhadra looks at the old man trying to converse with the silent cat which is not responding to him but the panther with tears looks at old man and slowly turned towards Bhadra, a huge roar and old man turned back, it was a lion running faster with its troop upon the soulless animals on the ground, he found that few lions are heading towards them, old man looked at panther it almost closed its eye, unfortunately, old man with a sad face ran towards the passage to climb, the lions ran around with no clue and the lonely panther with wound and tears slows surrounded by the blaze that yields into the aura of eternity, some are burnt, few were burning and some were yet to burn but very few seem to be against it,

Old man wiped his sweat, Bhadra looked at the huge burning tree in front of the gate and kept moving slowly looking at the fire that is continuously burning around, meanwhile, he found a few flat structured stones that were thrown by them, Saagar makes out that Bhadra kept recalling gradually he turned towards Saagar. Saagar bends his head with the guilt, old man noticed a small gap between the gate and the huge wall he walks towards the gap and turns back to the boys behind who are gazing at the ground and a few stones in their hands,

"This way, hurry up...! It's getting dark" says old man,

Saagar throws the stones from his hands and grabbed Bhadra's hand and started to walk slowly toward the gate,

"We don't have time to walk slowly, we need to rush as soon as possible to my house and I need both of you to help me water a few burning spots out there, hurry up...!" says old man,

Saagar pulled his hand then tries to walk faster,

"Do not leave my hand this time...! Hold tight when I am running" says Saagar and holds Bhadra's hand with a proper grip and started to run moderately towards the gate and gradually came out of the gap to the highway,

Old man slowly walks faster and started to run towards the slope on the highway to his home, Saagar looks at Bhadra every few seconds while running,

"Running on a highway like this is so exhausting..." says old man with a lack of energy,

Boys were left behind! After a few minutes of continuous run, Saagar looks at the old man standing near the slope, once reached Bhadra inhales faster and looked at the deep slope,

"Why are you guys so late?" asks old man,

Saagar turns to old man with a tired look and also inhales faster,

"Okay, get down soon..." says old man,

Saagar sat down in front of the steep and picks Bhadra upon him and slowly slanted in the slope,

“Remember the way I did...!” shouts old man,

Old man starts crawling in the steep behind them,

Bhadra smiled... Saagar was amazed looking at the rare reactions of the unspoken soul, Bhadra feels very happy for a roller coaster kind of swing in the steep, wet mud is revolting to their faces and he tries to catch the spiking mud on them, also the old man reached the bottom of the slope faster,

“Get up...! That’s it!” says old man from the behind,

Saagar opens up his closed eye and saw Bhadra's excited face in front of him,

“You are a kind of wonder, I promise when you start speaking you will be an amazing person,” told Saagar,

Old man from a few meters away,

“Come fast...” shouts old man,

“These kids are too hard to manage! And this disaster in front of me!” murmurs old man,

Saagar holds Bhadra’s hand and smiles at him and Bhadra responds with a smile too, a gracious which brings their lost energy and also helps them to forget the regretful incidents dipped out of misery which prepares them for a big future,

Tears of Hemavati, a fire that met couples, fears of guilt, and the unsung pain of mistakes lashes out as clouds to express its love to the entire village,

Once reached, old man told the boys to pick up the buckets from inside the house,

“Dear, you should keep pulling the water from this well,” says old man to Saagar

“I will show you how,” says old man and demonstrates to pull water from the well next to his house,

Bhadra kept observing both ramping around pouring water to the plants that were occupied with the red flower, old man picks up the water from the buckets trailed by Saagar, and a huge thunder once again starts piercing in the cloud which hits strongly to a spot on hilltop then few places up there started burning, the only thunder that shocks entire village, a giant cloud that is covering the multiple hamlets,

“God of thunder please don’t do this to us, this is not the right way to show your love for us, we haven’t done anything for you to get angry, everyone who leaves here is innocent why do you want us to cry? We always loved you God” said the old man with tears in his eye, he lost his energy and keeps the water bucket aside and sat in a place where he stood,

Atrai accelerated harder to reach the hospital as fast as possible, a scream of the burning couples inside the vehicle kept increasing and the employees tried to convince them to bear the pain and fight with it for just a few minutes, the burnt woman says,

“You can't save us...! We are meant to leave this earth...!”

The heartache makes out a tear for the workers next to them, Atrai at the front heard the painful manifest of women and he began to wipe his unstoppable tear, words from the women cease him from concentrating to stick on the curve roads, his mind echoes with those words by women, Cheyyar looked at Atrai losing his path and the vehicle is slowly turning towards the footpath, huge thunder that hits at the hilltop with a white flash that explodes in the sky following with a giant sound wave hits Atrai consciousness and swiftly rolls over his vehicle on being towards the footpath and everyone turned out to watch the big chain of thunder spreading in the sky to the unknown alley, Cheyyar blocks his ear upon the scaring thunder sound, burnt birds in the van shivers for the flash and the amplified sound wave,

Students stood in front of the scary house, heard the magnanimous thunder, every life in the school stunned for a while, moderately everyone turned towards the flying hill, a chain of lightning strike walking in the sky like a shining earthworm, eyes that wowed gazing at the huge lightning chain, accompanied by a sound wave that forges some to close their ears, without any hurry a white beam that occupies the entire school with the interval of eye blink then slowly fades down to normal leaving everybody speechless.

SHRUNKEN DOT BIRD

Rolling wheel that carried a precious life which burnt with the balance of fortuity, alike a disc in charge of saviors, one of the living bridges between the burning couple and a promised land, maybe the future of new dot bird, Atrai in the van expeditious like rapid lighting on the road with a prisoner of time who flies abruptly, the path which only had tree's passing are now gradually replacing with few houses, seemed like they are very close to the city,

"I think we have almost reached the town!" said Atrai,

"Yes, this is the start point!" says Cheyyar,

"How many kilometers we are left to reach the hospital," asks the Atrai,

"I am not sure about the kilometers but we are almost nearby, take a right turn over here..." said Cheyyar,

Atrai took a long right and people in the van slowly tilted to their right but employees kept holding the couples firmly, yet the couples slightly shifted to their right and again shouted for the unbearable pain,

"We reached the town... In a few minutes we will reach the hospital too... please try to control" says employees,

The couple started to wobble harder, they broke out from sustaining the pain and starts kicking the employees,

“I think the pain has increased,” says the worker,

“It seems to be uncontrollable,” says another worker,

A couple kicked the workers too hard and they are losing their grip,

“Sir... Sir!!!” shouts the worker,

“What?” shouts Atrai,

“We are unable to control it! They have started to kick, so we are losing the grip, please make it faster” says worker,

Atrai looks back from the rear-view mirror,

“We are almost reaching guys, please try to manage, somehow control them... just for a few more minutes... we will make it possible,” told Atrai,

“You see that huge building over there!” Says Cheyyar and points at the green building,

Atrai bends his neck and looked at the building, a board up that says hospital! Atrai quickly took his vehicle directly inside the hospital dodging watchman at the gate, on-the-entrance he stops the vehicle and ran towards the warden and told him,

“It's an emergency! Bring the moving bed go... fast...” shouts Atrai,

Warden ran inside and brought the moving bed, Atrai unbolts the back door of the vehicle, a dark light outside with the red illumination of burning hills whip a ruby glare upon the worker and couples inside the vehicle, Atrai looked at the workers and kept gazing at the burning hills,

“What are you looking at, shift them to the bed, now!” says Atrai,

Couples were loaded into the moving bed, warden gradually moved it in the pace towards the doctor, people inside the hospital looked at the burnt birds and they were shocked and some left speechless to the painful scream of couples, Cheyyar runs with the moving bed meanwhile feels uncomfortable looking at the burnt faces very closely, a doctor from the room walks out and asks,

“How did this happen?” asks doctor,

“Doctor the flying hills have caught up with the fire, these couples were inside it...!” said Atrai,

“Flying hills on the fire?” asks doctor shockingly,

“Yes!” said Cheyyar,

Doctor looked at Cheyyar and turned back to Atrai,

“How's that possible?” asks doctor,

“When we reached it was too cloudy and we found frequent thunder hits, maybe that should be the reason!” said Atrai,

“Ok bring them inside,” says doctor to the warden,

Warden moves the bed inside the operation theater,

Atrai turns around and kept searching for something, workers and Cheyyar kept following him, Cheyyar speaks to workers,

“He is in search of something right?” asks Cheyyar,

“Don't know, let's keep following him...” said worker,

Atrai walks to the watchman at the entrance of the hospital,

"Sir I need your help immediately," asks Atrai,

"Tell me..." said watchman,

"I want to make a phone call to the fire accident rescue team, do you have the number can you dial for me?" asks Atrai,

"Sure... but before that... You are going to move your vehicle from here!" says watchman pointing at the vehicle in the middle of the entrance,

"Sure, why not," says Atrai and turns to his workers,

"Guys, come here... drive the vehicle aside," says Atrai to his workers,

"Come with me..." says watchman and took him to a landline,

Hemavati with her friends in the classroom crying a lot,

"I won't come to the event, I am not interested in this participation, leave me alone" screams Hemavati with tears,

Friends trying to convince,

"Ok, don't come to the event, but stop crying," says Hemavati's friend,

But she kept crying continuously without breathing properly, friends were left speechless, meanwhile, Tapi with devil makeup entered the classroom with Ashoka walking behind him, everyone in the class kept silent for a while, a few students practicing the song and some were dancing but some got amazed looking at the remarkable outlook of Devil, Tapi tries to scare everyone and few students ran aside, gradually he walks closer to Hemavati, she wipes her tears and looked up towards Tapi who stood in front of her with the Devil costume that looks too scary but Hemavati again lied down to the bench with tears,

"Hemavati I am sorry for whatever happened, but you have to come out of it and fight for justice, bad people who misbehaved with you are still happy but you are crying for not doing anything," says Tapi,

Hemavati did not respond and keeps crying,

"Hemavati you are a class leader and you should be the inspiration for our mates, fighting against the dark makes a true leader!" Says Tapi,

Yet no response from Hemavati,

Tapi loses his confidence but Ashoka from behind comes next to him and told Tapi to continue the same thing,

"Keep motivating her, you shouldn't be the first one to quit!" says Ashoka,

Even her friends kept trying to motivate her,

"Hemavati it's my first ever performance on the stage, I never got an opportunity to make it...!" says Tapi and kept looking at her,

"Specifically, every time this act is only restricted to perform by our seniors but somehow this year we got a chance, I want our skit to look be better than theirs... This is going to be a pride moment for all of our primary section to prove" says Tapi,

No reaction from a crying tiny bird,

"I'm not sure about this opportunity would again come to us, maybe from next year seniors will keep doing it," says Tapi,

"Do you understand? We don't get this chance, please listen to me..." says Tapi,

Hemavati stops her cry...

"If you perform this action on the stage, whoever misbehaved with you will surely be ashamed for what they did!" says Hemavati's friend,

Hemavati slowly lifts her head,

"Yes, you should be confident because you are not a victim, they are the ones right!" said Ashoka,

Hemavati wiped tears on her cheek and said,

"Do you know, the entire school is now probably aware of this incident, everyone will tease about this and everyone is going to badly comment about me... do you know how bad it feels!" says Hemavati,

"So what? Have you done anything wrong?" asks Tapi,

Speechless Hemavati,

"No right? Then why do you care about not doing anything wrong, if someone has misbehaved with you, it doesn't mean you have to suffer, you should make them suffer by being confident, incidents revise your survival but don't decide your life" says Tapi,

"Do you know what happens if my father gets to know about this?" says Hemavati,

Hemavati keeps her hands on her head,

"He will beat me for going inside the scary house without permission," said Hemavati,

"Permission?" asks Tapi,

"First of all, my father didn't want me to act for this skit, but I forced my mom to convince him, but now he is going to hit my mother along with me for not listening to him," said Hemavati,

"Do one thing you join with us for this skit now, I will talk to your father later once the event ends... however it wasn't your fault" says Tapi,

"No, I don't want to participate at all please leave me alone..." says Hemavati,

"I already told you Hemavati, it is the mistake of those devils inside the scary house... I mean the negative minded people and they will be punished by the principal... moreover they should suffer... not you right?... please understand you are the class leader and you set an example for everyone in the class and also to entire school" said Tapi,

But Hemavati seems not convinced,

"Ok let's do one thing... once your father comes to the school, all students from our class will try to talk to your father and convince him that it wasn't your fault... you were innocent... and the boys are already being punished by the principal... okay? Your father will be convinced for sure... now don't worry, join us!" says Tapi,

All of a sudden, Teacher Manimala from behind asks

"Hey! What happened? Hemavati..." asks Manimala,

Hemavati got scared, Tapi looks at the Teacher and kept quiet,

"Madam, some boys have misbehaved with her in the scary house," said Ashoka,

"You have the skit, right?" asks Manimala,

"Yes mam, I don't want to act," said Hemavati,

"Why?" asks Manimala,

"Madam, she is scared of her father!" said Ashoka,

Tapi is looking at Manimala, and she looked at him then he goes back,

"Who are you? What are you doing here" asks Manimala,

Tapi removes his Devil mask,

"Madam, I am Tapi, do you remember? I just attended the drawing competition a few hours ago" plead Tapi,

"Yes I know, what are you doing here?" asks Manimala,

"We both have the skit together, I came here to convince her to forget the accident and join us for the skit," said Tapi,

"Okay you leave for preparation, I will prepare her for the skit!" said Manimala,

Ashoka and Tapi left the classroom to prepare, Manimala gets closer to Hemavati and holds her cheeks... wiping her tear,

“If anyone comments wrong about you, bring them to me, I will make sure they get punished and you don’t worry... okay! You should learn how to defend the negativity, life has a lot of ups and downs for you, and we should prepare to be strong like a butterfly which fights on its own entire life, at the time of growing... While evolving... In every second of its journey in the air, every rebirth of it makes better, stronger, and big beautiful flutter in the sky!” said Manimala, Hemavati shakes her head with a tear,

“Yes,” said Hemavati with slight tears dropping from her eye,

“That’s my lovely darling, now go and get ready to shine on the stage, let the brightness project on all the darkness go...!” said Manimala,

“Take care of her,” said Manimala to her friends,

Manimala walks to the principal room and found a few organizers were are already notifying about Hemavati’s incident,

“I just spoke to Hemavati... We will take care of it, you guys proceed with managing out there!” says Manimala in front of the principal,

Organizing senior students depart from the principal chamber, then the Manimala asked the principal,

“Are we contacting Hemavati's parents?” asks Manimala,

“Did you speak to the student?” asks Principal,

"Yes, I just spoke to that child and she is ok now and nothing to worry about it, but let us once inform their parents," said Manimala,

"Sure, just now those students gave me her father's phone number, let me call him...!" said principal and picks up the phone receiver and starts dialing,

Kali picks up the receiver from ringing,

"Hello... Who is this?" asks Kali,

"Sir, I am warden from the hospital... A Van driver named Atrai wants to inform you something" says warden,

"Okay...!" replied Kali,

"Just a moment sir!" said warden,

"Hello, hi..." says Atrai,

"Yes, what happened," said Kali,

"Am I audible?" asks Atrai,

"Yes, you are clear tell me!" said Kali,

"There is a huge fire caught up in...." Atrai paused for a moment,

Atrai saw a nurse rushing toward him and disengaging from the receiver and nurse walked closer to him and told,

"The couples are no more...!"

Saddened Atrai gets emotional

"The fire has damaged their deep organs, we couldn't rescue them..." says nurse,

Women's voice is revoking as an echo in Atrai mind,

"You can't save us...! We are meant to leave this earth...!"

He tries to hold his head,

"You can't save us...! We are meant to leave this earth...!"

He tries to get distracted,

"You can't save us...! We are meant to leave this earth...!"

Nurse asked the worker to walk with her to clear the formalities, Cheyyar looked at depressed Atrai,

"Hey, that's enough of throwing the stone, come let's go climb go hilltop as soon as possible, we are already late, you know that," said Saagar,

"Wait brother, I just learned to throw the stone, let me try a few more turns," said Cheyyar holding the stone at the mid part of the hills,

Cheyyar in the hospital stood speechless and recalled him throwing the stones into the firewood near the couples, wipes his sweat with a worried face,

Kali is still hanging on the phone and screams,

"Hello..."

Kali was on the phone waiting for the response from Atrai then colleague Bhima walked to him and speaks,

"Sir..." called his colleague,

Kali let loose his phone receiver from the ear and turns to Bhima,

"Yes?" asks Kali,

"We just got a call from our families and we have been informed that thunder strokes are hitting very hard in the village, we are expecting a very bad rain like never before in the history of our village," says Bhima,

"Oh, gosh!" replied Kali,

"Yes sir...! Everybody wants to leave the office, can you please permit us to go home early today" said Bhima,

Kali is thinking,

"I am not supposed to but... even I have to go early for attending school event..." says Kali,

"Is your daughter performing today sir?" asks Bhima,

"Yeah, my daughter Hemavati is performing a skit today!" said Kali,

"Wow, that's great sir... even we are eagerly waiting to go home sir... a bit afraid of our family nothing much...! We suggest you take care of your family too since we are expecting a critical weather condition, sir..." says Bhima,

Kali kept silent,

“Just only for today sir... I hope you don’t mind, we all are waiting for your permission...” repeats Bhima,

“I can permit you, but we have received an emergency already, I'm waiting for his response,” says Kali and tries speaking on the telephone,

“Hello Mr...?” asks Kali,

A few minutes later,

“Hello...” Atrai responded in a down tone,

“Why don’t you notify me before hanging up the call man, I have been waiting for you so long,” says Kali,

“I am sorry for making you wait for so long, it’s a big scene here...” says Atrai,

“Tell me?” asks Kali,

“A huge fire caught up in the flying hills, I just brought a burnt couple from there to the hospital, unfortunately, they are no more... I don’t know how many lives yet struggling in the hills right now but I want you and your team to rescue the lives immediately!” says Atrai,

“Fire? It's supposed to be raining right?” asks Kali,

“The fire seems like no rain could stop it... Please listen to me, they need you guys” says Atrai,

Kali holds on to his head for a minute, a colleague observed him holding his head, and he feels suspicious,

“Okay,” says Kali and hangs up the call,

"What happened?" asks Bhima,

"Come with me," said kali and Bhima, both walked to the main hall,

As soon as Kali entered the main hall, he found a lot of workers waiting for his permission meanwhile few were chatting, some changing the wheels of fire engine vehicles, some working under the beneath of fire engine to test the leakages, and some sat in the driver seat with the door opened and laughing with their team members, some stood alone looking at their watches and some were having fried peanuts,

Kali claps to seek everyone's attention,

"Team...! Assemble," says Kali,

The entire team assembled in front of Kali, some are expecting him to permit half-day leave...

"I thought of letting you all go home early, unfortunately, it's not possible today guys... because it's an important day for all of us," says Kali,

Few started to murmur, and suddenly a big thunder strike to the metal roof, everyone got scared and looked up with confusion, slowly it started to drizzle outside the office,

"This is the issue," says Kali,

Everyone turns back to Kali,

"There is a big fire that has ignited in flying hills, I want everyone to unite at flying hills right away with all the fire engines we have...

come on... load your vehicles with full of water and inspiration in you..." says Kali,

The team gets energized with little confidence, but Kali found few members were getting scared looking at the white flashes and slow drizzle with a powerful full wind that floats away many dried leaves on the ground,

"No matter what... nature deemed us to be part of its activities, we are responsible for many lives out there... that is why we are here right... when people need us... what if your family needs us?" asks Kali,

Every colleague looked at him...

"No matter what, we all are with you..." shouted employees,

"Yes... Rescue every life that struggling in the hills, two fire engines will go to the hilltop, one at the mid part of the hills, and one at the bottom" says Kali,

Alike soldiers firefighters prepared themselves with confidence,

"Myself with few members will start to turn off the fire from the bottom of the hills," says Kali,

Kali at the entrance stops Team A and B in the vehicle and guided them on different routes to the flying hills and explained a few secret paths at the hilltop, then Team A and B departed from the office to the flying hills,

"Be safe..." shouts Kali,

Kali walks to his truck and sat in the front seat next to his driver Mahi by then he found his watchman running toward his fire engine through the mirror,

“Yes?” asks Kali,

“Sir... A call for you from the school” says Watchman,

“My Daughter right, inform her that I might not come to the event, and also inform her to leave school early with her mother,” told Kali and looked back towards his team onboarding,

“Sir, it's principal... She said it's very important!” told watchman,

“Inform her that we are into a big emergency!” says Kali to watchman,

“Ok sir...” replied watchman,

Kali departed from the office,

“The sun has almost gone for sleep and the darkness rising,” says Kali looking at the window,

He got to see the hills covered in smoke with a red light, he tapped Mahi’s shoulder and told him

“Speed up!” said Kali,

“Don’t worry sir, Team A should already be there...” says Firefighter,

“We might get assistance from the clouds!” said Kali,

Fire engine rushing in zig zag roads which tilts the whole truck, Kali grips himself with two hands and gets a very cool breeze with a slight drizzle drops on his face, blitzing red smoke in the flying hills that seems like a wrap of big challenge to overcome, burnt particles in the air, streamed to the front glass glaring the driver Mahi's vision, few seconds later the speeding fire engine enters a road that is completely filled with flying fire dots dropping down slowly Like a snow, entire road brightens up with the orange light, the stunning view mesmerizes everyone in the vehicle, Mahi opens his mouth and looks up the flickering tiny fire spots from the sky then he decelerate the vehicle unknowingly, everyone left speechless, Kali pulls himself out of the window and tries to catch the fire dots that's floating in the air, few attempts later... he got to grab a fire dot in his hands comes back to his seat and quickly opens his heating hands then tries to blow the air from his mouth to turn the blaze off... it was a burnt butterfly...

Kali gets choked with a unique kind of shock in his mind and turns to Mahi, he looks at Kali's hands and enlarges his eye with tears...

A burnt butterflies rain!

"All those fire dots in the sky are butterflies, caught with fire on them..." said Kali,

"From the flying hills" replied Mahi and wipes his tear then clutches his truck to the next gear, the truck wheels start to revolt faster,

A group of small girls walked on stage with a mic...

Small girls Chorus...
Give us the bravery to wish everything right,
Give us the bravery to express and fight,
For honesty, for goodness, for justice and truth,
Give us the bravery to choose goodness in youth,
Give us the bravery to be calm when we are wrong,
For faith, for knowledge, for freedom and to stand one among.

Small boys Chorus...

We owe you for caring for our school with blessings of protection,
We thank the survivors who loved us with the bundle of appreciation,

Help us to speak with honesty and equality,
Help us to smile with modest and adversity,
Help us to overcome the reserved and racism,
Help us to step up who is deserved in individualism.

We owe you for seeking our love with reliance,
We thank the love birds who spread warmth with a family of gods,

Small girls Chorus...

Give us the ability to forgive and help,
Give us the ability to look at the dream and fortune,
For the promise, for family, for love and friends,
Give us the ability to motivate and drive,
Give us the ability to participate and thrive.
For you, for me, for us and the world...!

Small boys Chorus...

We owe you for the wonderful world you have made for us,
We thank the world who believes in love that still exists...

Tiny students received great applause from the crowd and they left the stage,

Another girl walked into the stage with a mic

"Good evening all of you... Your presence here illuminates a prominent love towards our Five Elements School,"

"Guess who is next... let's clap for our historical and well known all-time best skit from our school..." the host girl shouts,

The audience slowly started to clap...

"The fading wings of the town..."

The audience raised to clap and whistle,

"A story of beautiful butterfly and the craving infernal soul...." says host,

"Woo...." up rearing audience,

"ART OF ASSASSINS AND SORCERESS...," said host,

"Woo...." shouts audience and whistling,

Lights turn off slowly, a ghost quiet for a while, the echo of a baby crying and mother trying to hush him down in the crowd, a sound of pulling chairs to backward and front, gradually the lights turned on... soothing grassland and the bright glossy flowers... Hemavati walks in as a stunning monarch butterfly on the stage,

"Woo...." cheering audience,

People hurried up to adjust themselves on a chair, some stood looking at the colorful stage,

"Hi...." shouts random children at the event,

A lot of stunning and colorful butterflies entered the stage and flew around with an impressive flutter all around the place gazing at the glossy flowers,

Wings that covered the student legs impressed adults with a real feel of butterflies fluttering everywhere, butterflies on the loop fluttering together with a melodic hum that fascinates the whole crowd,

Hymn...

Loading from the rainbows...
Melting like a shade...
With a life that mounts around, had to breathe...
...
...
...
...
Rain bending sparkles...
Jolting with pain...
With a twinkle that shallows, unrolled a champion...
...
...
...
...
Sail like an unseen... hover...
...
...
...
...
Sail like an unseen... angle...

A very sharp hymn that reached many audiences in the event left speechless and mesmerized, and the glitters falling around from all the butterflies on the stage spread to the audience around, also to the children at the bottom kept jumping to catch some glitters dropping all over the place,

While the glitter drops towards the ground like a few butterflies drop themselves on the nectars of the flowers in the garden, some left happily flying around with a significance of its kind,

An unknown devil that saunters in the garden noiselessly, Butterfly Queen in the sky looked at him heading towards their troop on the nectar, the unpredictable devil starts running in the garden shouting around with a dreadful noise scared the butterflies to its vital core, Butterfly Queen drops herself from the high rumbling down rapidly, distanced of a high-speed wind that hauls everyone at the bottom, devil looked up at the giant Butterflies shifting to the bottom with a powerful wind that seems attentive,

Butterfly Queen slowly hovered in front of him with large wings of hers,

“You seem to be Uninvited, Unclear, and Unwise...!” says Butterfly Queen,

A dangerous red eye...

A negative caricature...

“What’s your problem...” shouts Devil with a base voice,

Butterfly Queen flew a cent back and bends her head for his scream and lifts her head with confidence,

“You seem to be annoying!” said Queen,

“Who are you...!” shouts Devil,

"I am Butterfly Queen... I am here to protect my kind..."

"Seriously...?" laughs Devil,

Butterfly Queen kept swinging her wings slowly in front of him with no response, looking at his demented nature,

"From now on, I am the king for all you...! Get used to it. Obey my orders, this place will be mine from this moment!" told Devil,

A few butterflies up on the flower got up and starts flying in the air,

"Until my announcements, you do nothing," says Devil,

Queen was about to respond, by then one of the butterflies came to her,

"Queen, as per your suggestion we have found a large flower land that suits our entire generations to survive for a very long time," says tiny butterfly,

"Do we have freedom?" asks Butterfly Queen,

"We located some of our kind," says tiny butterfly,

"What kind?" asks Butterfly Queen,

"We only found morpho, nothing apart from them," says tiny butterfly,

"Great. Our lineages! Then it should be okay for us to reposition" says Butterfly Queen,

"Fine, lead everyone to the new flower land, I will follow your signals," said Butterfly Queen,

“Yes, madam Queen!” says tiny butterfly,

Butterfly Queen turned to the Devil with a smile,

“Fine, please enjoy your garden for the rest of your days,” said Butterfly Queen,

Devils looked at her confusingly,

“I meant. This place is all yours from now onwards” told Butterfly Queen,

“Oh, Wonderful, thank you!” says devil,

Tons of butterflies in the sky wandering towards the new land, Queen hovers toward the flower with a thanking gesture,

“Hey flower, you have been a goddess!” says Butterfly Queen,

Flower smiles back,

“We mean it!” says Butterfly Queen,

“It’s our nature” responded glossy flower,

Devil looked up and tons of butterflies in the sky flying towards a new empire, he turns around at the evacuated garden seemed like essence that are slightly fading after the absence of butterflies, Devil with confusion looks around then he found Butterfly Queen hovering in front of the glowing massive flower, for a while he kept looking at the Butterfly and his confusion face slowly turns to a negate smile and walks to her,

“Hey...” says Devil,

Butterfly Queen with no response looked at him,

"There is a saying about the colors from your wing!" asks devil,

"I beg your pardon!" asks Butterfly Queen,

"Color from your wings signify forge of luck to others who get it," says Devil,

"That's when you own it but seek intentionally the luck should be a curse instead" replied Butterfly Queen,

"How about surrendering me one of your butterflies from the troop, so that I let you all stay in this garden itself!" said devil,

"That's hypothetical! However we are leaving this place as we do not require this garden anymore, we have found a new empire itself!" said Butterfly Queen,

Devil gets offended seemed to fail yet reflects to be elevated, Butterfly turns around towards the flower,

"I will keep coming here to visit you," says Butterfly Queen and steadily fastens waving her wings,

Reckless Devil pulls out a big sword, laughed vigorously, and cuts the Butterfly Queens' wing!

Light goes dark on the stage and the audience is left in shock...

Between a dark silence, the suffering voice of Butterfly Queen screeched in the pain, a very sharp sound which piercing to the inner souls of the audience with an immersive sadness, and gradually Devil's laugh increased with the sync lights turned on, Audience got serious, the Devil sitting in front of the Butterfly Queen and a lot of butterflies flying around him trying to attack nevertheless it hurts him, reechoing palette filled on his form, Butterfly Queen's wing left as faded regardless of the infuriating form of the Devil wiped the color on her wings to the core by disarming from her flying abilities, A struggle of a survivor, a tear for her few last breaths, Butterfly Queen with one wing seems to depart from its soul on the ground screeching with severe pain, blood on the ground reflects her one wing to possess as a two wing yet it's just a reflection,

Very large dark clouds form in the garden above the devil and butterfly queen, students at the back struggled to hold the cardboard sheets painted as dark clouds and the boys kept moving left to right with less energy, due to that audience started clapping and laughing at it, Absence of guilt yet with a great existence of arrogance kept him laughing again and again in front of a fading soul, Butterfly Queen looks at him laughing and turned towards the bunch of butterflies with tears, trying to jab him but which left him with no harm yet increasing his boldness to misdeed, the light turns off again at the stage and a student narrates a short story,

Once upon a time, perhaps two billion years ago, divined as last moving tree on earth kept having a ball of its final days in the sea shore, in spite of that a furious caterpillar came out of the egg and starts eating its shell making a crispy noise on his shoulder branch grabbed attention; on its swing caterpillar finds a classic greenish leaf and kept eating later with no direction crawled entire tree and the tree kept looking at the interesting life kept wandering around, as soon as moonlight arrived the significance of silent shades that streamed in as a rays that brought up a brightening sparkles, meanwhile the creatures who wakes up in the realm of blinking stars, in pursual of sustain flying beasts kept gazing the world that retained inaudible on the sunset, caterpillar was scared but the tree kept looking at its feeling and awaits for the next situation, some beast kept attacking and some tries to eliminate, the scared caterpillar with sweat moves faster to find itself a place to hide but always a brilliant beast finds it, caterpillar with no option shreds the tear looking at the moon at the end of its life, unexpectedly a strong shield around it created and suddenly shelters inside by the time flying beast gets disappointed and flew away, tree gets amazed with its sudden super power and felt excited about it to see more however he waits for a very long time looking at the sacred caterpillar covered with pupa, he kept missing his tiny cutie pie, and awaits eagerly on the sea shore looking at the never-ending sea and sky merging together at its end, on a very hot afternoon a cold wind breezes around the sea shore then the caterpillar slowly cracking out its pupa, and the tree gets very excited and kept looking at one of its branch. A caterpillar with an Arc Angelwing broke out from its shell and slowly wiped its stuck wings with one of its legs and starts flying! Tree was stunned with an awestruck experience left occupied looking only at the butterfly fluttering in every part surrounded by air at seashore and slowly flew in the beach and kept going towards the end of the sea merging to its sky and the tree kept looking and expecting her to return but the saddened tree bends his head with disappointment, something he senses and lifts his head and all the birds on tree swings away, he found the butterfly returning with tons of butterflies along with her, the mob with unique colors and pattern reflecting the sea as a rainbow tint, the tree kept gazing at it with a wonderful experience on its lifetime, slowly all the butterfly makes a hymn and passed above him, animals and other creature heard its signal and kept running behind tons of butterflies, tree left with a suspicious feeling and he turned towards the sea then found a big tornado from the sea heading towards seashore that seemed to devastate minimal lives, few minutes later the tree vanished in the waters along with few unspoken lives, the butterfly signal that helped few lives on survival of next generation!

Lights turned off on the stage and followed by regular lights and Butterfly Queen returns with the flashback, lying on the ground looking at the Devil,

"We are meant to be the survivors of great disaster, few but much of annihilations which cannot harm us!" says Butterfly Queen,

The Devil kept laughing, she struggles for a while but got up with the tears but she fell again, constantly Hemavati as a Butterfly Queen tries to pick herself up and fall into the dust, his laugh motivates her constantly, she brings out a little energy from her one wing that glitters and took a strong stand in front of him alike soldier,

"Mr. devil you have made a mistake cutting off my wings!" said Butterfly Queen,

"You have disarmed my wing, yes... But along with your destiny!" said Butterfly Queen,

Tapi behind the Devil mask sweating and gets a bit serious looking at her vibrating wings yet she stood strong in front of him, a few seconds later he increases his laugh again,

In a base voice, he spoke,

"This is where your destiny lies, you might be the survivor, I am a self-seeker!" said Devil,

Hemavati looks at her wings and shreds tears and turned back to him strongly,

"This universe is predestined while a bright overcomes the dark and kept repeating every day"

Devil walked around her,

"They say that a conflict between lives starts below the two rays that never ended, and I am nowhere to bring a change to this timeline that dark can walk in the light as the light always did in the dark!" said Tapi,

"Do you believe that powers hold the superiority?" asks Butterfly Queen with tears on her face,

"Affirmative" replies Devil,

Butterfly Queen lifts her head to the sky with the tear that formed a lot of clouds...

She hits the ground with one wing and jumps up rapidly like an arrow towards the sky, and hovers to the higher clouds,

"You believed in getting her wings which you got and she believed in something now it will" screams tiny butterflies around him,

Devil gets shocked and turns here and there looking at the sky, the wind starts blowing faster, trees and plants swing heavily to its left and right,

"If you believe then nature will walk with you," said tiny butterflies,

Devil confusingly looks at the Queen hovering inside the passing thunder, after a few minutes she did not turn up, Devil starts laughing again, and he looks at the crying butterfly troops and told,

"It's your turn now... my brilliant pets," says devil and walks to them,

He keeps harming trying to catch the tiny with his powerful swing and he is faster than the butterfly's dodge, one of the tiny butterflies gets injured and fell to the ground, devil kept stomping it by then it saw the Queen at the sky rotating like a tornado along with the cloud that's emulating the thunder, tiny shreds its tear with a smile looked at Butterfly Queen but with no response, bright-eyed Queen from the sky swifts towards the ground striking upon the Devil!

Slowly the stage lights turned off, and the audience started to clap a few seconds later again the lights turned on and a new generation with a new Butterfly Queen for the troop and all are humming,

A flap that lifts our lives,
With the waves that made our paths,
A world that made us bright,
Reflections were on the height,
Every mortal in mountains,
Always wished to fly,
Await for a few returns of light,
Wings that would have built-in them to live like all butterflies...

Fly higher like all butterflies,
Fly like a stroke of luck, fly like the faith of trust,

A color that builds a lust,
Waves are a rage of thrust,
A world that gave us smiles,
But the flower that hides in style,
Unknown evils around us,
Knowingly wants to see us cry,
Wasted crying hours of life,
Happiness would rush like a rainbow in our lives,

Fly higher like all butterflies,
Fly like a stroke of luck, fly like the faith of trust,

Performers at the stage assembled in a row and bowed down to the audience,

“Awesome” shouts the audience and the increasing claps,

"That was one astonishing performance by Hemavati and team!" said host walking into the stage and told to clap,

Kali claps,

"What are you guys still doing here?" asks Kali to Team A and B that stood at the entrance of the flying hills,

"Boss, all this time we struggled to turn off the fire that caught on this big tree in front of the gate and we are now almost have pulled it aside," says Rihand lead of Team A,

Kali claps again,

"Fine, make it fast!" shouts Kali at the entry of flying hills,

Within a few minutes, Team A and B pulled the tree to a corner,

"Okay you guys, leave...! Don't forget to rescue the lives out there!" says Kali to Team A and B,

Team A and B rush to the hilltop,

"Be strong and super-fast" shouts Kali to the roving Fire engines,

"What are you waiting for? Entertainment? Get the Ropes!" screams Kali to his driver Mahi,

Mahi ran to turn the generator on. Water pumps with a force from the tank, Kali holds the pipe firmly towards the burning path and sideways of the entrance gate, slowly kept walking all around the burnt places and found large burnt board consisting of road map to the flying hills, but partially burnt! Kali looked at the half information on the map and kept watering, Mahi from behind shouted,

"Sir there is a small path next to this gate you should have a look at it, seems like too much of a blaze inside!" said Mahi,

Kali turned with the water pipe in his hands,

"Follow me at the passage on the reverse! I will march ahead watering the burnt places!" said Kali and enters the path,

The tired old man stood for a while next to the well, Saagar keeps pulling the water out of it and filling it into the bucket, old man and Saagar pushed themselves to the core and many spots that are watered are now producing the smoke that annoying to breathe for the lives inside the forest, but the aggressive fire kept increasing, the tired voice of the old man told,

"If you want, get a break for a minute child," said old man to Saagar,

Suddenly a puppy behind shouts and sprints near Bhadra, Bhadra stood up and kept running around the ashes, Saagar shouts,

"I can't lose you again Bhadra, you have to stay here," says Saagar strictly,

The puppy ran towards Saagar and jiggles around his legs faster, old man looks at the cute puppy and smiled, Saagar laughs and pushes the puppy away and told Bhadra to take care, Bhadra picks it up and the puppy had a burnt spot on it, Bhadra wipes it and shows the wound to Saagar, Saagar looked at it then picks up the water bucket and poured them on the puppy, suddenly the puppy starts dropping its temperature, its blood seems to be getting colder then it starts shivering,

"Why did you pour the entire bucket of water on it?" asks old man,

And old man grabs the puppy from Bhadra's arm and rubs the head then took it inside his house and drops it inside the wardrobe covering it with wool. Wobbling puppy sleeps tight inside the wool.

Netravati waited for a long time in front of the gate anticipating Yamuna and Krishna's arrival,

"Oh, they did come in the bike right!" Netravati asks herself and looked inside the school,

"I think both should have entered already!" murmurs Netravati gazing towards the stage,

"Let's go inside and look for them once" murmurs Netravati,

She walks in looking at a huge crowd inside the school event, Teacher Manimala walks to her and stops

"You are?" asks Manimala,

"I am the mother of Tapi" replied Netravati,

"Great, then you are Tapi's mother!" says Manimala,

"Yes, you know him?" ask Netravati,

"Yes, such a bright kid, please make yourself comfortable," said Manimala with a smile,

Netravati smiles and thanked her and kept looking around for her sister in the huge crowd but she couldn't find Yamuna or Krishna, found a chair at the corner and she sat behind inspecting around and turned towards the stage, then a small girl was host below the bright rays honoring the awards for the winners participated in various activities, top rankers one by one starts entering the stage to collect their awards, the audience clapped and Netravati claps with no concentration but until the host said,

"We request for Tapi to come and receive his honors!" says Host,

"Please give a big round of applause for the best painter of the year!" says Host,

Netravati sat too far from the stage where Tapi looks very short yet with happy tears and a respectful slow clap on his collection of the first award, Netravati feels very proud at moment and emotionally excited,

Lots of burning trees behind keeps falling, while Team A kept heading towards the hilltop, Team A driver Purna stops the vehicle, a tree keeps burning rapidly on the road has blocked their way, Team got down immediately and watered it, as soon as they beat out the fire a guy from Team A stops the vehicle and people came out from the truck and found continuous roadblocks by heavily burning trees following to the hilltop,

"Oh, my God!" says Purna,

"We don't have any other option, we have to set down all those burning trees and progress to the hilltop," says Rihand,

"Then we might be late to reach the top sir?" says Purna,

"Yes, obviously!" replied Rihand,

"People up there?" asks Purna,

Sad faced Rihand responded,

"We will try to do something, get the truck fast," says Rihand,

Rihand told his team to walk with him with the water ropes,

"Let's make it fast..."

"We are running out of time..."

"Keep watering only on the burning tree on the road, and the rest boys will lift it aside and keep moving ahead"

"Remember do not drain out, we need them on top!" said Rihand,

Purna stops the fire engine in front of a burning tree and kept wondering at the burning hilltop, and dark forest surrounding them slightly burning, and unusual ghostly voices hanging around but he couldn't notice any of them,

Old man walks out of the house and seems to be ready to water the burning spots again, he comes out and found Bhadra sitting next to Saagar, but Saagar kept pulling out the water from the well at little intervals, old man walked toward him to pick the water tubs meanwhile he heard a sound from the burning passage, he got to see a man stuck in the passage trying to come out, old man picks up the water tub and began to throw them towards the passage, a man filled with dark smoke around him, while Kali walks out with the orange reflecting dress and holding the water gun, turns off the water and walks to the old man,

"Hey old man, I am Kali head of the fire rescue team," says Kali,

Old man smiles at him.

"A man from this place had called, seeking help," said Kali,

“We are eagerly waiting for you and we need you up there,” says old man,

Slowly a very big fire engine rushes out of the passage in front of the old man’s house, Saagar holds Bhadra’s hand the walks near the truck, and kept gazing at it,

“Don't worry, we have a lot of teams that have already left to the hilltop!” says Kali,

“You guys have bought Hope!” responded old man,

Kali hugs him and told,

“Chill, it's our duty, can you guide me, old man!” asks Kali,

“Sure,” says old man and locks the house door,

“Please follow me” stated Kali,

“Can the truck enter?” asks Kali,

“Yes, there is a forest route to the hilltop, villagers do use it,” says old man and started to move,

“This is the best route for us to get into the core part of the forest that is raging,” says old man,

“Follow... Follow... us...” shouts Kali to his driver Mahi and rubs on the head of Saagar and Bhadra then kept moving ahead with old man,

Mahi turns the Fire engine to steady and slowly crawls to the entrance of the forest route, Kali turned on the water gun and starts to spray at the entry of the forest route which is burning heavily,

“From what time this place is burning?” asks Kali,

“More than three hours” replied old man,

“Did those couple stuck here?” asks Kali,

“They were from the passage,” said old man,

The sound of the Fire engine, water spray, and the burning tree is immense where the conversation makes out to be inaudible yet they kept shouting,

“Just a moment... Did you know them?” screams old man,

Kali looked at him and again kept spraying,

“The couples” screamed old man,

“I got the call from a person who led me here and told me that doctors couldn’t save those couple and asked me for help!” screams Kali,

Disheartened old man bends his head and holds his face for a while and few seconds later wipes his eye and tries to be normal and thought of speaking to Kali, but he couldn’t express himself due to the heavy noise of the fire engine, water spray and the burning environment makes him mute but not his mind,

“Those couples rushed asking me to save their life” murmurs old man,

“I did try very hard, but...” murmurs old man,

A tear rolled on his cheek like rolling snow from the peak of a mountain, and he kept wiping it continuously,

Kali bends his head from a streaming exhaust of the blazing woodland, few minutes later the initial path of the forest route watered completely and the fire starts reducing at the entry, Kali stops spraying and gets back removing his face shield and wipes the sweat looking at the old man,

“Temperature is too high in there...!” said Kali,

“Yes, do you need some water?” asks old man,

“No, thank you!” responded Kali and looked at Saagar and Bhadra sitting on the ground,

“Who are those boys?” asks Kali,

“Students came to visit the flying hills, but they got stuck near the gate for hours seeking help,” said old man,

“I see...” replied Kali,

“That tiny boy there... was lost! I went up there and found him, thankfully! The fire was just beginning then!” says old man,

“Gosh” murmurs Kali,

“I’m going to suggest you a good idea, let them sit in the truck and come with us to the forest,” said Kali,

“Yes, it should be good” replied old man,

“They will be safe in front of us,” said Kali and wearing the mask to enter the forest,

“Hey, Boy!” shouts old man,

Saagar got up and walks toward old man,

“Both of you, get inside the truck, as soon as possible,” says old man,

“Yeah!” said Saagar,

Saagar walks to Bhadra and grabs his hand and took him to the truck,

Fire engine driver Mahi looked at both seriously and told them,

“Keep looking around for any burnt lives from the window!” says Mahi,

As soon as the truck entered the forest route, Saagar starts turning his head left and right analyzing the burnt logs and the smoke-filled environs,

Lohit lead of Team B has put his head out of the window, noticed a lot of burnt woods were flipped aside,

“Maybe Team A has cleared the obstacles for us,” says Lohit looking at the smoke emitting burnt trees on the roadside,

“Sir, look there...” says Team B driver Damodar and points toward the mid part of the hill,

The biggest fire that is burning on the mid part of the hill, Lohit takes a deep breath looks at it, and said,

“Be prepared for any kind of scenario, I’m not sure what is going to happen if in case, nature is not happy with us! Every single decision taken by us will be very crucial today” says Lohit,

Magnanimous fire god slowly calms down at the entrance of the forest route in the flying hill, smoke in the dark mountain unites with the cold breeze of the evening, Saagar at the window seat gazing around, Kali grips the water pipe in two hands and sprays at heavily burning spots, old man behind him holds the water pipe assisting him to move at ease, meanwhile, Kali heard the noise of someone moving behind the firewood but he is unable to identify anyone, he turns back to the old man and told,

“Can you check with the driver if he did see anything over here!” says Kali,

Old man leaves the water rope and walks to the truck,

“Saagar, did you get to see anybody from up there?” asks old man,

“I couldn’t see anybody, but felt a movement,” said Saagar,

“Ask the driver,” says old man,

Driver heard him,

“No, I didn't” replied driver Mahi,

Old man walks back to Kali and told,

“They didn’t spot any activity,” said old man,

“Okay, maybe we could find them after turning off this fire,” says Kali and turns over the water pipe to zig-zag and tries to spray all around him,

Old man drags a water pipe from behind and slowly moved step by step while Kali ahead spraying some spots to get normal, Saagar and

Bhadra got down from the fire engine, Saagar holds Bhadra's hand and told him,

"Do not leave my hand, you keep following me! No matter what, stick with me!" said Saagar,

He holds Bhadra's hand and walked in front of the fire engine and the strong orange headlights of the truck blend with the smoke and made the path visible brighter, old man walks to Saagar and asked,

"Why did you both get down?" asks old man,

"I heard some steps sound again, it's somewhere over here!" replied Saagar,

"Is it!" said old man and looked around,

"Come let's find it," says old man and walked with the boys,

Kali looked turned back and watched, old man with the boys searching for something, and moves ahead spraying continuously,

"Is anybody over here!" shouts Saagar,

"Please speak we are here to save you!" said old man,

A peacock lying at a huge plant that has built itself as a cave with lot of insects and other companies inside saving themselves from the fire, its colorful feathers have burnt to half and faded, and damaged legs that shivering, yet the peacock tries to shake its leg creating a sound to hint someone to seek help, eventually, the peacock couldn't lift itself had tears in its eye and feels like,

The world that is burning,
Every step that was swallowing,

A smoke that blinded and seek to blend with,
Flying rescuers pass over the luck and stood at myth,

Bhadra could connect with the mysterious sound, and his mind voice originates,

“We are failing to search and it's very near to us,” thinks Bhadra,

Bhadra was kept dragged by Saagar who was holding his hands, yet he kept looking around as faster as possible,

“Every assassin who tried to flare was once dealt the wind that blown, every dream that was buried, one last life had resolute for a reason” Bhadra’s mind voice,

“Please wait for me to find you, try to hold that final breath, hold that dream you're trying to give up, we don’t try to blind ourselves it was the time that we’ve been followed by sins” Bhadra’s mind voice,

Peacock from a small gap inside the plant cave looks at Saagar and Bhadra in the orange smoke light searching for something,

I could never get into the abyss carrying the godly color in me,
Only the red that found me to bleed,
He had my legs that held my destiny,
The sound that connects everyone to crawl towards the gate of God!

Peacock kept shaking its leg very hard and trying to create a sound of it, Saagar, Bhadra who is nearby moving slowly and looking around, but couldn’t make out the right place, A tear from peacock touches the ground... then it stops shaking its leg,

“The sound stopped!” said Saagar,

“Yeah...” said old man and kept walking,

Peacock looks at old man and the vision slowly gets blurred...

"Okay boys, let's go... The sound stopped! It might have gone" says the old man and walks back to the truck,

"Did you find anybody?" asks Kali holding the water gun towards a huge burning tree,

"We were hearing some sound, but we couldn't find anything!" said old man,

"Even after searching for a long time?" asks Kali rotating his water pipe zig-zag towards the blaze,

"Yes, a few minutes later the sound stopped, hence we returned," says old man,

"Oh?" replied Kali and feels strange,

Suddenly a huge sound resonates from the hill top, Everybody left speechless and looked up at the sky, a rampant out of the sky pops up... the only historical tree for the village, known for more than three hundred years and a tree that many family generations worshiped at, unfortunately had caught up with fire and slowly falls down with a sturdy hit, Bhadra tries to wave his hand to clear the smoke that is suffocating him to breath and tried to lift his head to see the magnanimous sound but he couldn't tilt his heads up, he forced his neck by pressing from thumb and kept trying to lift his head up but he couldn't, with no option he looks at the ants rolling upon the burning trees in front of him and kept wondering at the water flowing rapidly from pipe connected to the truck, a chain of water beautifully splashing to the fire on dry grasses on the ground, few seconds of water spill that formed a tiny water pond upon the ashes eventually reflecting the hill top, Bhadra slowly gets closer to the standing water and the reflection led him to envisage a huge burning butterfly slowly flying towards the sky waving its continuous blazing wings that creates a huge sound of burning flap, astonished Bhadra sights the fire butterfly dropping the tears and entering inside the cloud, the tear dropped to the reflecting water below his feet,

"Hey, it's raining! says Kali,

old man looks up and a raindrop falls to his forehead,

"Finally! We are getting help from the god itself" says old man,

Drizzling raindrops with not much desired to turn off the blazing fire in the hills,
Thunders that help as flash for everyone's vision at forest,
Unstoppable fire melted the woods into ashes and trapped many lives,

Kali moving with a water pipe in his hand, tilting them to right and left,

"We still have a long way to push," says old man,

"Don't worry, I think my team has reached there" replied Kali,

"I have deployed two teams, one will start pushing from the mid part of the hills and another will take care of the hilltop," says Kali,

Suddenly a small deer shouts in a mild voice that no one heard, Kali turns back with the water pipe and directs water toward a small rock cave that is burning heavily, Kali increased the water flow level in the gun and splashes near the rock, within few seconds the fire turned off, a small cute deer below the rock,

“Is that pig?” asks old man bending his neck and trying to look at it properly,

“No, it’s pudu,” says Kali,

“Can you just help that pudu out of the rock?” says Kali,

Old man walks closer to it, by then pudu fawn ran away from the rock striding upon the water, Saagar and Bhadra inside the fire engine looked at the cute Pudu jumping down towards the gate,

“Did you see that Cute little Pudu fawn, it had wounds in its leg yet jumped upon the heated ashes with the tear, running away wishing to live further, to find its path of survival!” said Saagar in Bhadra’s ear,

Team B in full swing has started to water the burning spots at mid-part... Team A enters the hilltop crossing many roadblocks by then a burning doll hits the front-rear glass of the fire engine, Purna got scared, smiling doll's face seems burning looks nightmare,

“Purna, turns on the wiper,” said Rihand,

Wind at the hilltop is faster than regular, ruined hilltop had no rain, no human, Team A began to spray water instantly at the hilltop,

Team B found a building which is heavily burning,

“Can you hear the sound?” says Lohit,

“Yes sir, I could hear a lot of people's voices from the inside,” says Rescue guy Manu,

Lohit starts to spray the burning building while again he heard a murmuring sound from within, he turns to his colleague Manu and told,

"Again, I heard a voice of someone from inside, I am sure that someone is stuck inside, get in with our team, ASAP," says Lohit,

Manu from the team gets closer to the burning building and found a board that's written as OUTSIDERS NOT ALLOWED, he turns around then keeps moving, all of sudden a medium-sized burning butterfly rapidly flew out next to his ears, Manu dodges and turned back looking at it, a butterfly flew faster flapping its wings back-to-back to get rid of the red devil upon it, unfortunately, the half-burnt butterfly hits the burnt tree and falls on the ground shaking its wing slowly and leaves no sign of alive,

"Hello... is anyone in there?" shouts Manu,

"Please respond, I am here to help you..." shouts Manu,

Nobody turned up, yet a murmuring voice from inside kept resembling, as soon as he entered, a huge burnt wooden roof falls in front of him, diffusing a mist of ash along with tiny firewood spill inside the building. One big room with large stands assembled with glass bottles filled in with different colors, some interesting extracted fluids that are glowing in the dark, he found a glass shelf that is locked, walks closer to it then lifts himself with his toe and found an amazing collection of butterflies kept in it as a showpiece, none of them were alive but it looked real, kept gazing at few more unique colored and rare designs of butterfly that never seen before in any parts of the world,

"This place seems to be a butterfly farm or? Is it a lab?" he murmurs looking at all the glowing butterflies inside the glass bottles,

Team A gets afraid looking at the shops raging with the fire on the hilltop, Rihand informed his team to find the lives at risk,

"Wait," says Rihand,

He looks around at the dark spots and told his team,

"Take the torch from my bag, it should help you!" says Rihand,

Team B kept spraying the building but fire the seems to withstand and keeps raging itself from within, Manu inside the building kept listening to a murmuring sound and keeps moving further in that direction by crossing small burning logs on the floor, few minutes of search at every corner of the lab yet he didn't find anybody, meanwhile he found a door that seemed locked, he suspects and walks to the door and keeps his ear to the door when he heard the mysterious sound-alike papers rubbing on the surface,

"What if a lion inside?" asks himself,

"He wipes his sweat looking at the door with heart beating faster!" murmuring Manu,

He kept thinking for a while,

"We don't have much time, let's do this!" murmurs Manu,

He opens the door!

In a complete darkroom, scared Manu stood near the door and kept looking in to find anything,

"Hello?" shouts Manu and wipes his sweat,

One butterfly in the dark, glows with a light on its wings with a stripe illumination and slowly flutters out of the dark with stunning movement, the butterfly flew around him he turns left and right while it hovers in front of his eyes, an astonishing cute butterfly with a reflection of colors keeps rotating for some time and swifts out of the lab faster by dodging all the fire blocks, again the mysterious sound from the same dark room, he turns back to the darkroom... One by one, thousands of butterflies illuminate its wing and creates a bright radiance inside the room, Manu gets astounded for a minute kept looking at butterflies with different colors yet flapping their wings at the same time and staring at him, Manu passed down his throat and wipes the sweat looking at it, all the butterflies in the room start spreading and rushes out of the room, then he found a lab worker who left unconscious at the corner of the room, he covers his face and slowly walks inside towards the fainted person,

Manas searched all around the hilltop with the help of a torch, got to find some cows struggling between the slopes and burning plants around it that lead them to shout, he manages to set the flames down and gets the cows to the safer side, unfortunately even the safe zone catches with mild fire below the grasses,

Manu from Team B walks closer to the unconscious person in the darkroom, lot of butterflies kept rotating inside the room and some flew outside, Manu sat down to the fainted person and tried shaking him to wake up, and looked at his identity clip on his pocket states 'SENIOR RESEARCH DEPARTMENT',

"To save you, I had to walk upon thousands of partial dead butterflies, you took them here to research and experiment, but you now lied down along with them," says Manu,

And he picks him up on his shoulder with no option had to walk again upon the butterflies that laying on the ground,

“I’m somewhat feeling like there are a lot of babies under my shoes which are trying to breathe and I’m walking upon them...

Team A succeeded to turn off the burning plants near the cow, Manas directed the cows near the truck and asks Purna to look after the unspoken lives, then they walked away with the torch,

Senior Researcher retained at the front seat of the fire engine! Manu walks to Lohit,

“I found a scientist who was fainted inside,” says Manu,

“Fine!” says Lohit and continues to spray at the building,

“Seems like the building has lit very strong, by the time I turn off the fire at one spot and change the direction, it reproduces the blaze again from within,” says Lohit,

“It is going to be harder then?” asks Manu,

“I think we need backup in some time!” says Lohit,

“Fine, give me some time I will return with one last observation inside the building,” says Manu and entered the building,

Team A enters a pink light decorated lane with the continuous stalls that are burning heavily, a very mild thunder passing above them, meanwhile the hard-hitting wind that keeps pushing the rescuers backward, the water diverts from its flow and the light poles broke down, moving leaf's in the air tries to convey something that no one could understand, greatest message from a tree swinging to left and right, a connection between the nature and other lives around it has a hint that left unleashed, but the rescuers might imprison the destiny of few more lives, rescuers passed ahead from the burning stalls and inspecting one dark spot with the help of a torch, where lot of plants around has a blue and green glow and a whisper from within, Manas the rescue guy from Team A feels unusual and kept looking at it with directing his torchlight for a minute suddenly a baby starts crying and a mother tries to calm, he starts moving slowly pushing the plants aside, he gets down to a moderate slope which is actually an unknown path nobody knows where it leads, he swings his torch left to right and keeps walking over the plants that gradually gets tall as he slowly got down, they now cross above him, as he gets closer. Makes out by hearing a few people's conversations,

“Mostly, we found some people trapped over here” murmurs Manas and walks upon the plants,

“Have patience... I am there” says mother,

“Don’t worry we are there with you” said a man,

As he got down too much low from the hilltop slowly the moonlight fades from his surrounding, and he turned back to his teammates a few kilometers upwards from him, running around to turn off the big fire at the continuous lane stalls, the water spray from up that is drizzling towards some bottom parts of the hills, and the Manas down here gets wet then his colleagues near the stall couldn’t manage the situation kept reminding him for help but manas looks front while the baby starts crying again,

“Seems a lot of people trapped in here, I think they need me!” murmurs Manas and kept moving towards the trapped people,

Rihand shouts,

“Manas, you will be fired out of your job if you are not reporting here immediately,” says Rihand,

Manas stops moving ahead and heard the command from his lead Rihand, he bends his head with the regret and slowly steps back to the stalls at the hilltop, few seconds later his team starts to scream his name back-to-back and the Manas began to run faster towards the hilltop,

Manu entered the butterfly farm, glowing butterflies brilliantly depart from the lab, Lohit with the water pipe trying hard to turn off the magnanimous blaze from the lab, but gets to see a chain of butterflies gradually one by one fly outside left speechless,

"Oh my god, rare ones!" says Lohit,

Manu enters the lab and stood near the door looking at heavily burning stands that had glowing butterfly wings and colorful chemicals,

"Seems like, the entire lab is lit up" murmurs Manu,

He is unable to move further, he kept looking around and sense no activity but seemed like the large stands inside the lab could fall one by one cause a big disaster then he found the glass shelf alike showcase next to him that consisted of live unique butterflies as a collection, he breaks the glass and puts all of them in his pockets and few on his hands ran out,

"Hey, what's in your hands?" asks Lohit,

"I found some preserved butterflies, let me keep them in the truck," says Manu and left them inside the truck and walks back to his Lohit,

"These butterflies were inside all this time?" asks Lohit,

"Yes, this place seems to be a butterfly farm," says Manu,

“Okay,” says Lohit and kept busy watering the building,

“Such unique butterflies right?” asks Lohit,

“Yes sir, nowhere in the world we could find such rare butterflies,” says Manu,

“This is not working... It's waste of time, no use of trying to water it from outside, I think we need to get inside the building to turn this off” says Lohit,

Team B gets closer to the lab,

Saagar inside the fire engine looked at the increasing rain and kept his hands out of the window, all of a sudden, the track bends to the left off-road that almost getting close to the ground, Bhadra and Saagar fall upon one another but Mahi again gets a hard right that stabilizes the truck back to normal, old man stays behind for walking slowly holding a big leaf upon him to avoid getting wet in the rain, Kali pushes himself faster to the front and reached an empty ground, where he could see one side of the bottom hills wasn’t caught up with the fire and has too much of rain pelting, then he turned up at mid part and hilltop had no rain but a red smoke flowing to the sky, at some point! After a few minutes of marching, Kali found Team B's truck and someone lying in the front seat, he ran towards it and tries to talk to him, but the fainted person did not wake up Kali found a card in his pocket that stated ‘senior research department’, then Kali turns towards the burning building and walks to Team B unit that stood at the entrance of the building while getting closer to the building he looked at a heavily raging fire rupturing out of the doors and the side windows

“Maybe the chemicals inside the lab elevating the fire stronger,” says Manu,

"Yes," says Lohit,

Kali looks at the explodes from a burning building, gets panic, and starts running towards them, truck comes out of the off-road and slowly moved towards Team B's truck on the roadside,

"Is everything okay?" shouts Kali running towards them,

Lohit turns back and found Kali running toward him, then walks back from the door,

"Thank God you are here, do we have water backup from your truck Sir?" asks Lohit,

"Yes, it's on the way" replied Kali,

Lohit increases the water pressure from the water gun, and the water splashes inside the building, Team C truck arrived with Saagar and Bhadra inside, Kali whistles his truck,

"Come to the front," says Kali,

Mahi surpasses Team B truck and gets closer to the burning lab,

"Oh my god, look at this building. Burning so intensely" said Saagar,

Bhadra looked at the burning lab. He gets a flash from one of his drawing books, suddenly he holds his head and started screaming,

"Dear, what happened?" asks Saagar,

"Saagar is he alright?" asks Mahi and kept looking at him screaming,

"He looked good all this time, what happened to him all of sudden?" asks Mahi,

"Unknown issue! It disappears after a few minutes..." replied Saagar and tries to hold his shoulder to calm him down,

"Take care of him, I will be back soon..." says fire engine driver Mahi and got down from the truck,

Mahi preps in front of the burning lab,

"Is this the same head pain you had afternoon?" asked Saagar,

Bhadra kept screaming due to the severe head pain meanwhile a mist of flash forecasting in front of his eye, one fine day lot many butterflies in the main hall of his house flew in the air, and one by one soul departed inside a frame of mysterious gods, Saagar picks the water bottle lying next to the driver seat, Bhadra did not remove his hands that holding the head,

"Bhadra, please drink the water, everything will be alright," says Saagar,

Rihand and other mates scolded Manas for disappearing without information,

"Where were you all this time?" asks Rihand,

"I heard some noise down there," says Manas,

And points his finger toward the lower forest from the hilltop,

"Did you find anyone?" asks Rihand,

"No, by then I heard your voice and returned here!" says Manas,

"Fine, after this will go there!" says Rihand,

Kali gets on to the sideways of the lab and starts spraying the windows,

Bhadra and Saagar slept lying on each other's shoulders in the front seat and Kali watered the lab from aside and looked at Lohit, who stood at the entrance for a very long time, Kali walks to him

"Are you scared to enter inside the building?" asks Kali,

"The door has been blocked by a large wood log, I'm unable to find a way inside," says Lohit,

"Follow me!" says Kali,

Then he increases the water force from the pipe and sprays at the entrance and told Manu to jump inside,

Raging blaze upon the stalls has slightly reduced, Manas helps the team holding the water pipe, slowly a large group of glowing butterflies flew from the bottom of one side to other direction, the team gets wowed looking at the unusual activity at the hilltop, Manas in the team noticed that the butterflies were directing towards the downhill where he headed a few minutes ago heard a voice of a baby crying and a mother,

After a long struggle Team B and C have turned down the fire in the lab which looks savage as hell, smoked as unwell, Kali walks beside the large burnt stands fell inside the lab,

"We were once brought here for an educational visit... I was around fifteen years old then," says Kali,

"At that time, this place was the only factory in our county to farm butterflies with rare patterns, once entered inside... We were able to see tons of butterflies flying around, they were modified to their best formation to represent the world's largest butterfly farm with unique collections" says Kali,

"Oh, was it that beautiful? Wow..." says Lohit,

"Unfortunately, it seems destiny has loaded with uncertainty towards the lab sir..." says Manu,

"Yeah, it's regretful to envisage such a lively place turning into a history now!" says Kali,

Tired old man took a long time to reach the lab, he found a person standing out of the lab, he walked towards him and asked,

"Where's Kali?" asks old man,

"They are inside," says Mahi,

Old man stood near the door and looked at a large steel stand turned into a black dye, as soon as he entered, he coughs very badly due to the extensive smog inside the lab, holds his breath, and walks back to the entrance,

Rihand grappled restlessly against the fire at the beginning of the slope at the hilltop, the fire element at its last stages to show up in hills, also the flame is very low but it has occupied wide space that continued to expand its rage and the wind that seems disturbing the flow of water from the gun, he had to struggle more intelligently to cool down its rage, Manas drives the truck towards the slope to help Rihand on reaching wide-range burning areas, but he gets distracted looking at the butterflies that flowing in a sequence, he puts down the brake and stops the truck at one place where Rihand could reach maximum area to spray the water then Manas got down from the fire engine and went after the butterflies,

Kali keeps walking in the lab and found nothing else after investigating the place for some time,

"Let's get back," says Kali,

"Okay sir," says Manu,

"That new guy in our team, heard he is your close friend?" asked Kali,

"Yes sir, he is Manas...! My childhood friend! Very brilliant, he kept asking my referral for years to join this job" says Manu,

"Oh, Manas and Manu... akin Name! He waited for years?" replied Kali,

"Yeah, he waited for a reason, he wanted this role... in saving someone's life defines a great job! And it is kind of working under the god he always says and believed this Sir!" says Manu,

"Wow, what have you said, I never thought of it!" says Kali,

"It's true right sir!" said Manu,

"It is, in which team is he now?" asks Kali,

"He went with the team that made it to the hilltop," says Manu,

"Sounds great," says Kali,

All of a sudden, some screechy noise that pops out from the behind, everyone turned back, it was full of smoke-filled surroundings and an invisible butterfly hovering in the smoke flying up and down, Kali and Manu looked at it interestingly,

"Sir, did you notice," asks Manu,

"Yes, I did, it looks so beautiful, but where is this fly, is it an invisible kind of butterfly?" asked Kali,

"Even I'm not sure sir... A few hours back when I came in, it was completely burning, I walked in to see if someone was stuck, but all I heard was mysterious voices, I opened a door somewhere here, then I got to see a room full of butterflies flying around with unique lights on its wing and some were dead in the ground, those butterflies were very unique in color and it was glowing, I also found a senior researcher fainted on the ground" said Manu,

"God, is it?" asks Kali,

"Yes, I took him out," said Manu,

Kali walks ahead waving his hand in the smoke and gets closer to the invisible butterfly hovering in the smoke, a very small wing flattering in the smoke faster, Kali lifts his hand to touch the beautiful then the tiny fly kept rotating around his arms and slowly disappeared,

Gradually the smoke inside the lab decreased and they found a glass door to a room and a person inside struggling to come out and kept waving his hands continuously,

Manas kept following the paths of butterflies, the truck he left behind is slowly slipping downwards to the slope, Manas in the path of dark and deep insides of the forest kept moving together with the spiked plants, at one point all the butterflies flew near a glowing stone, one by one they started to rotate like a tornado moving towards the sky, Manas ran towards the stone by then all the butterflies got disappeared, Manas kept wondering looking at the dark red sky but desolated, apart from the smoke traveling everywhere, he looks at the glowing stone and a script written on it,

“Set to release the giant butterfly from his existence can never be elected but to take place when a calm gust of uninvited negativity inward bound enchanting towards many lives awakens the giant to produce a huge blow of airstream with magnificent sparkles in the direction of the special to amend whole mob destiny”.

Manas wonders about the meaning of the script and he talks to himself while reading the message,

“Set to release giant butterfly from his existence can never be elected? I am not sure of this line, but to take place when a calm gust of uninvited negativity inward bound enchanting towards many lives, is this line highlighting the fire which is targeting many lives in this forest right now? Yeah, I think it is the fire, the negativity of today's evening for us in this forest... Ok, what’s the next line, awakens the giant to produce a huge blow of airstream with magnificent sparkles in the direction of the special, I did not notice any giant awakened over here blowing any airstream, to amend whole mobs' destiny. Where is the mob who is amending it? No this is an old script I cannot link this to the current situation” murmurs Manas,

“I don’t think there is anyone stuck over here, it's better to go back and help our lead Rihand instead of following strange things on this hill” murmurs Manas and ran back to the fire engine,

Rihand with the water gun all alone kept struggling for a long time to turn off the raging fire at the slope of the hilltop,

Manas kept running faster wiping his sweat, suddenly he heard the voice of the same crying baby, he picks up the torch from his pockets and looked around, slowly walking upon a small rock with light from his torch an empty area then he tilts his torchlight downwards, there were two hundred tourists with their luggage and few with children, they have already built wooden shelters for their children from getting wet in the rain, they've put smoke to avoid the mosquitos, they have made beds with cloths tying it to the trees, few ladies together preparing the food, within few hours of the trap they've arranged themselves with a better civilization strategy and Manas looks dumbstruck at his position,

"Airstream with magnificent sparkles in the direction of the special to amend whole mob destiny". Was that stone trying to convey something to me? Okay, let's not worry about it right now, let's plan how to escort this huge mob from here, GOD!" murmurs Manas,

He stood up and walks in front of the rock and forms a noisy whistle, people from below saw this person standing on the rock above them, some had a tear in their eyes and got up looking at him like a god appeared from the skies.

MOUNTED WOUNDS

Fly that came in smoke invisibly, wasn't it a messenger for us?" asks Kali to Manu,

"Yes sir, which led us to save all these people inside the lab," says Manu,

"I did sense an unusual situation looking at the butterfly in smoke because earlier to this I had experienced something like this" Manu,

"Yes, this is the specialty of flying hills," says Kali,

Team B and C get closer to the glass door,

"Sir, I think we should break it?" said Manu,

"Yes, we don't have any other option apart from breaking it," says Kali,

The door seems easy to break but eventually, it is the opposite, Kali, Lohit, and Manu tried to put a lot of pressure to break it, but all of a sudden, from a nowhere the old man walks in with a big stone on his shoulder and shouts

"Move!" shouts old man,

Everyone steps aside, the person inside the glass door ran backward, old man threw the stone at the door lock handle, it was slightly damaged but didn't work well,

"Don't get too excited" says Kali to old man,

"Get back sir," says Lohit to old man,

Kali and Manu started to kick the door back-to-back putting all of their energy, into the broken door handle slightly helping them to unlock it, everyone gave a strong push to it and then it opened, the dark smoke from inside erupts outside, Kali, old man, and Team B entered inside the glass door

"What is this room?" asks Kali and walks inside a clearing smoke,

Gradually the smoke is reducing inside the lab room and they found a bunch of employees lying on the ground, and one who stood near the door walked toward him,

"Thank god you turned back to my sighs," said employee,

"Is everyone alright?" asks Kali,

"No, due to a lot of smoke from the inside, none were able to breathe and they fainted, we need to hospitalize them immediately," says employee,

"Okay!" says Kali

"Team, come on... Start loading everyone to the truck immediately" says Kali to the Team,

Rihand ties the water gun to his hip and firmly climbs on the slope, he pauses in the middle of climbing and noticed the fire engine kept skidding backward, Rihand gets scared and his heart beats faster,

"What the hell, where did he go again?" murmurs Rihand,

He kept his leg on a small stone under his feet, he grips himself standing on it and climbs faster,

Manas got down from the rock and walks in between the large number of tourists who remained in the forest of the hilltop,

“Sir, please take us out from here... We tried very hard to get out of this place, every path is burning to its heights, and we do not know a way to home” says few men with children on their shoulders,

Granny walks towards him with a giant leaf and some food in it,

“Son, please have this,” says granny,

Manas took the food that is too hot, he blows the air from his mouth and walks ahead,

“Let him sit,” says another person,

Manas sat upon a suitcase next to him and had the food,

“Why don't you all join me,” says Manas,

Everybody rushed towards the old couple with giant leaf for food, they made themselves a queue and one by one came with food and sat next to Manas, next to him a baby in the hanging clothes tied to a tree got up and starts crying, a mother in the queue leaves the giant leaf and ran towards her baby, Manas got up holding the leaf of food from one hand and swings the baby and told mother,

“You get the food, till then I will look after him!” says Manas,

Mother smiles at him and went back to the queue then the Manas swings the hanging cloth and he tries talking to the baby,

"Sweetie, what's up... what is your name" speaks Manas,

Some of the men who completed having food joined in serving others in the queue, some made their spots to sit with their family and friends to have food,

"From when are you all stuck over here?" asks Manas,

"We came to the hills in the afternoon," says a young beautiful girl named Dravyavati,

"How did you guys end up here?" asks Manas,

A Boy named Daya next to Dravyavati speaks,

"We came in a jeep along with some other travelers, the jeep person left us here and informed us to make use of two hours for the refreshment at the hilltop and he mentioned of picking us once he returns with new passengers to the hilltop, but none showed up here..." said young boy,

Damodar with his daughter on his lap, speaks to Manas,

"At some point, the rain started, we thought the jeep drivers would return after the rain stops, but the rain stopped! No one appeared. Some tourists did not wait, they tried to walk down but they noticed some spots were lit with a huge fire and they ran back to the hilltop with no other way around, and those thunder strikes? That was the insane man... The stalls got lit badly. What not we did face! The way that old age people got panic. How all we ran here and there trying to save our children, it was very tough!" says Damodar and wipes his continuous rolling tears,

"One person took initiative and bought us all to this place, but we were not sure how safe is this place too, every second it seems like we are walking upon the broken bridge above the fire, we shouldn't have come here!" says Damodar,

"Sir, let me tell you one thing. No matter how many fire engines may come to save you, if the coordination within you is missed? It's of no use! Initiatives at the dangerous situation with the right planning matters a lot" says Manas swinging the baby in the cloth,

Mother comes with the food and lifts her baby to feed, Manas throws the leaf aside and washed his hands from the rainwater,

"Everyone, feed yourself as much as possible, it's a long way to go home!" says Manas looking at everyone with a positive smile that brings hope,

Gentlemen have saved plenty of animals risking their lives,

He looks positive that brings the same ambition for everyone that they had earlier while entering the hills,

"It's completely hell out there, the roads are blocked with huge trees, the raging fire at several spots, we do not have enough vehicles to transport this many people from the hills, still how many are stuck in other spots we are unaware of it, if other teams are survived safely not sure and don't know how to get all these people and the animals out from here safely" murmurs Manas and looks at happy faces staring him back,

"They seem to be looking at me as their savior, let's not try to fail their fortune losing our confidence!" murmurs Manas and convinced himself with positivity,

Bhima, driver of a second fire engine in Team A bends himself and looked inside the slope for the continuous voice of someone shouting, later he found his lead Rihand running towards another truck of theirs that was located in front of him, Rihand sighs to Bhima asking to get inside the truck and stop it from skidding, confusingly Bhima looked at him and slowly turned towards the truck then it was slowly going backward, shocked Bhima enlarges his eye and jumps to the seat holding the steering and starts the fire engine immediately and moves forward, as in Rihand runs behind the truck and Bhima took the fire engine to the main road and stops, Rihand comes to him running,

"Thank God you came! Buffoon left the truck and disappeared again" says Rihand,

"Oh my god, that newly joined guy?" asks Bhima,

"Yes, how's the thing up there?" asks Rihand,

"Yes, we have almost set down many spots sir," says Bhima,

Manas walks in front of the mob,

"Hello everyone... Please maintain silence, I need all of you to listen carefully... The reality is, you all are from different places and it takes a lot of time for everyone to reach their houses, there are a few issues that you need to understand first. We do not have enough vehicles in this town to vacate everyone at the same time, we will be able to transport only a few batches at each round, we don't have any other option other than walking all the way downwards to the main road" says Manas,

Everyone looked at him with no response,

"We would save a lot of time if we start walking right now!" says Manas,

Everyone seemed to be demotivated,

"Don't worry guys, the needed one will be shifted on priority" says Manas,

"My mother can't walk, she is too old to make it" shouts women in the crowd,

"That's what I told you right now! We have few vehicles for now, where we can start vacating the needy one's one priority to their houses" says Manas,

"How safe is it to walk in this dark while the hill is still burning and the animals are at high risk, where can we take them?" shouts another man from the mob,

"We have few trucks on this hill, they are at various spots working to turn off the fire, and which is now almost decreased, we might face very limited problems which can be solved by us, you have made this for living in such a less time, then things are possible by us, trust and walk with us," says Manas and turned back to the crowd again and told,

"We have so many gentlemen over here to protect us! Do not worry... Tight up your shoes, let's leave" says Manas,

On a dark and cold evening with little light from other sources unable to see each other's faces in the mob and Manas found some men and told them to escort the crowd in the front along with him, a few at the back and sideways to cover everyone and respond immediately to any issues arising from the crowd, everyone pushes themselves to right and left forming a big chain,

Team B and C loaded all fainted employees from the lab inside the fire engine with the available space,

Kali walks out of the burnt lab and found the team kept loading the fainted ones,

"Haven't you guys finished yet? Make it fast!" says Kali and walks to the Mahi,

Mahi woke up Bhadra and Saagar and told them to sit at the corner adjusting with other passengers, by then Kali comes to him and told,

"Take them directly to the hospital without any deviation and try to be fast!" says Kali,

"Sure sir!" replied Mahi and starts the fire engine left the mid part of the hills immediately,

Old man walks to Kali,

"Can you send some of your team members with me to the forest up there, I will have to find out if there are any complications on the other parts of the hills" says old man,

"Definitely!" says Kali,

Lohit with his team walks with old man towards the forest, Kali walks down with his colleagues to the main gate of the hills,

Rihand walks with the Bhima near the stall and found half burnt toys, butterfly candies, dark butterfly key chains, highly smoke emitting plastic boxes, house decorating items in the shape of butterflies lying on the ground,

Bhima calls him,

"Sir, please come... you have to check this," says Bhima,

Bhima took Rihand to the corner of the hilltop, and pointed towards the road below them,

“What is that? Something is glowing in a row?” asks Rihand,

“It’s a group of people walking towards the main road with a long firewood,” says Bhima,

“We need to get to them as soon as possible,” says Rihand,

“Yes Sir, they might need our help,” says Bhima,

Kali walking with his colleagues to the bottom meanwhile heard the siren sound from one of the fire engines that went to the hilltop, he turns back then he found a truck turning at the edge of the mountains and some roads are glowing with an orange radiance that defines route of hilltop brighter,

“Let's keep moving, they will have to pass us,” says Kali,

Kali with his teammates kept moving downwards, his colleague told him,

“Sir, someone is walking with the firewood in the hand, look back,” says teammate,

Kali turned, a guy in the dark with firewood in his hands walking down with a huge chain of people behind him, as he gets closer, his teammate told,

“Sir, he is a newly joined person,” says teammate,

Manas nears with a smile,

"Nice work, I never expected a great job from a beginner, you have made us all proud!" says Kali to Manas,

Team A vehicles nearing the mid part,

"I think even your team is arriving here," says Kali and looks up at the fire engine horning behind the huge chain of people,

Kali walks to the middle of the road as soon as the truck gets closer and swings his hand, swiftly the truck dashes near Kali and stops,

Manas with a pang of guilt looks at his lead Rihand sitting in the front seat behind the glass, Rihand got down from the fire engine looking at him with an angry face,

"Where had you been? You could have informed me before taking any decisions, right? We were searching for you up there!" yells Rihand,

Kali interrupts Rihand from scolding him,

"Let's appreciate him, look at this people, he has done a great job," says Kali,

"Sir, he left the truck behind the slopes when nobody was around, the truck was skidding to the bottom, thank god the Bhima responded for his irresponsibility," says Rihand,

"A truck for Million people or Million people for a Truck?" asks Kali and Rihand,

Rihand bends his head with no reaction kept quiet,

“Whatsoever, taking a good decision without anybody's permission at a critical time also needs great strength, I appreciate your spontaneous reaction,” says Kali,

One by one starts clapping to Manas, he gets a motivated looking at a lot of positive energy,

Kali told Rihand to pick up the lost tourist in the truck,

“Drop them to their respective places and get the busses while returning to the hills, we have a lot many people to vacate,” says Kali,

“Sure sir,” says Rihand and left with a few old aged tourists in his vehicle,

Bhadra in a sleepy mood in the front seat turns with a dozy eye and found a tourist next to him who smiles and rubs his head, Saagar shouts from outside,

“Bhadra wake up!” says Saagar,

The fire engine gave a stop near the school gate, and Saagar holding the school gate and waving his hand towards Bhadra,

“Get down soon dear!” says Mahi,

“Careful,” says Mahi and passes on in the fire engine,

Saagar and Bhadra entered the school gate with a scared faces crawling inside, a lot many people drenched in the rain yet talking to their children with a smile, Bhadra walks looking at the ground that had tons of funky hats filled with colorful feathers and some with a vivid form of animals, Tapi from far away observed Saagar and Bhadra entering inside the campus wondering at the audience, spontaneously ran and pushes Saagar with an impactful pressure to his shoulder,

“Sorry, Tapi!” said Saagar while collapsing backward,

“I told you not to take my cousin to the hills,” says Tapi and ran to punch him,

By then, Tapi’s mother Netravati found him fighting with his classmates, ran towards them, and stops from brawling,

“Tapi... Stop it! Says Netravati,

Tapi looked at his mother and smiled at her, and hugs her with a smile,

“You shouldn’t do that to your classmates darling, ask him sorry,” says Netravati,

“He took Bhadra to fly hills even after my warnings!” says Tapi,

Saagar with a frowned face kept looking at Netravati,

“Just a second I will be back,” says Saagar, left Bhadra and ran away,

Netravati comes closer to Bhadra sat down then hugs him,

“Are you alright dear?” asks Netravati,

Netravati wipes dye spots on his face,

“I am unable to find your mother and father, they should be somewhere over here, let’s wait for them,” says Netravati and keeps turning left and right and rotates her eye faster,

“Oh Yes, probably they might have stuck in the rain somewhere in between,” murmurs Netravati,

“Mom, shall we take him to our house today, please,” asks Tapi,

“Yes, come to our house, I will drop you back tomorrow morning,” says Netravati to Bhadra,

Bhadra with no response quietly looks at the students holding their parent’s hands with unique colorful hats, Netravati picks up Bhadra, carried him, and starts to move holding Tapi’s hand,

Kali got down from the fire engine in front of the school and walked inside then looked at Netravati carrying Bhadra, Kali comes to her and said,

“Your son is a great hero, you should be proud of him,” says Kali to Netravati,

Confused Netravati did not answer anything but she smiles with a doubtfulness,

“He had slipped inside a deep burning slope in the flying hills,” says Kali,

Shocked Netravati looked at Bhadra and gets tears and kisses him,

“Thank god, my dear,” says Netravati,

“We saved them no issues but these boys later helped us to rescue some animals that were struggling inside the forest, they are a hero for many lives today!” says Kali,

Netravati felt proud and kissed Bhadra again,

“If your mother gets to know about this! Then she will be very much proud” says Netravati with a smile and slight tear,

Saagar few meters away looked at Teacher Manimala talking to Kali standing with Tapi’s mother and he walked toward them, Kali looked at Saagar as he was nearing him then smiled and turns back to discuss with Manimala,

“This guy, I was talking about,” says Kali pointing at Saagar,

Everybody turned towards Saagar and his parents behind him,

“Such a wonderful active kids, they just followed as we guided them to do,” says Kali,

Tapi in a shocking state said,

“Hi,” says Tapi,

“Hey Tapi, how are you?” asks Saagar’s father,

“I am fine uncle!” replied Tapi,

“Thank you for saving our kids,” says Saagar’s mother,

Kali smiles at Saagar’s mother,

“He just told us what happened up there!” says Saagar’s mother,

“Thank you for everything!” says Saagar’s Father,

“No problem, it's our duty” replied Kali,

"Your kids were too good when the hill was dangerous as hell, these boys dared to walk with us! They are real soldiers" says Kali and appreciated them,

Then Teacher Manimala starts to clap,

"Great boys," says Manimala,

"Is this boy from our school?" asks Manimala to Netravati looking at Bhadra,

"No, he is not, he should be joining from next year," says Netravati,

"Okay! Great I will ask our principal to honor these boys with the appreciation" says Manimala,

Saagar gets closer to Tapi's ear and told

"See your brother has won an award before joining the school, just because of coming with me," says Saagar,

Tapi makes his face angry, Saagar looked at it then walks behind slowly,

"How about the situation right now in the flying hill," asks Manimala to Kali,

"We have almost turned off the blaze and started to vacate some tourists who were trapped," says Kali,

"Did anyone get hurt?" asks Manimala to Kali,

"Yes, the animals did but now we have arranged some doctors to medicate the wounded animals, we have a big Team arrived at flying hills," says Kali,

“Oh” replied Manimala,

“But I am sure it will cost a week to settle down,” says Kali,

“Oh my god!” asks Manimala,

“Yes, we will be operating twenty-four hours from today, until everything gets normal...” said Kali and looks at the dark sky, and everyone looked at the smoke from the flying hills reaching the sky and forming the clouds,

Principal holding Hemavati's hands stood outside her chamber, Hemavati looks at her father standing in the crowd and points the finger, Principal took Hemavati to her father... Kali looks at Hemavati walking with the principal and smiled at her daughter,

“That's my cute daughter,” says Kali looking at Hemavati,

Tapi and Saagar, turned towards the principal walking with Hemavati, the ambiance twirled silence as the principal walks closer, Kali observed her daughter's sad reaction,

“Where is your mother,” asks Kali,

No response from Hemavati,

“Didn’t she come?” asks Kali,

Yet no response from Hemavati, Kali laughs and asked

“What happened dear,” asks Kali,

“Please come to my office,” says the principal and took Kali and Hemavati along with her,

As soon as Kali entered the principal's chamber, Hemavati started to cry aloud, Kali tried to calm her down but she kept crying unconditionally,

"What happened madam? Why is she crying so much?" asks Kali,

Principal turns back with a serious face, Hemavati goes silent,

"I don't want to see you crying again, does that make sense?" says principal,

Hemavati got scared and tried to wipe her tears and trying to control her emotion and walks with Kali,

A wing that was faded into ashes bought its raiser towards flashes,

A sail that averts souls toward the innermost of its love that flamed brings their descendants bond to evade,

A dark boat that one could spot floating in their evening, it's been said that one could wait for that train of heavens arriving below the shadows of the moon,

Dark sorrows emerge in the veins of a smiling friend who ushers one to forge a zeal from within,

Netravati carrying Bhadra and holding Saagar's hand walks in the freezing moonlight that seemed like known darkness, mist-filled mountains in presence of immortals who spoke to clouds that wail someone's tragedies and one's wisdom,

Many lives in flying hills, that arch beneath the sorrow of falling stars, the bus arrived at the entrance of the hill loaded with water bottles and food, the rescue team served the tired souls and the parents kept trying to calm their babies from shrieking but the freezing air penetrates everybody's sense of flow, rescue team tried to motivate to fight against the tough times,

Netravati drops Bhadra in a chair, then looks at the house, which feels like a mystery,

"Tapi... groom yourself and help Bhadra also..." says Netravati,

Tapi and Bhadra got themselves showered and sat in front of the television, Tapi turned on the television and changed to a cartoon channel, Bhadra for the first time looks at the television and gets amazed, Tapi keeps laughing loud whenever a rat cheats on a cat, and all of sudden someone opened the door and Bhadra turns slowly and gets panic as in the door slowly opened under a dark sky with a thunder strike behind a man stood,

"Hi, daddy" shouts Tapi running towards his father,

Tapi's father Banas entered with a smile dropped his bag and gave a hug to Tapi,

"How was the function today? Did you get the award" asks Banas,

"Yes dad," says Tapi,

Banas turns and looked at a boy in front of the television and he walks toward him happily,

"Look at who is in the house," says Banas with a smile,

Bhadra did not lift his head but kept looking at a rat running for a cat's chase,

Banas lifts Bhadra from both hands and kissed him on his cheeks, Netravati walks out of the kitchen and told her husband,

“Get ready and come to dinner soon,” says Netravati,

Bhadra looks at Banas and feels like a very good and smart gentleman,

“Tapi... bring him to the dinner,” says Banas and leaves to get a shower,

Frozen winds wandering around the flying hills, a family that is eagerly waiting for their hearts to return, souls in the tears for their unaware relations are yet connected to the sphere. At an extended night, the landline rings which awakens Netravati at the house, she rubs her eye and walks to the landline and she picked up the phone,

“Hello? Who is this?” asks Netravati,

The house a ghost quiet for the moment,

“What!!!” she shouts,

Bhadra opened his eye in the bed and he turns slowly and looked at Tapi in a deep sleep, Banas coughs and asks Netravati,

“What happened Netra?” he says and grabs the landline receiver from her ears,

“Hello who is this?” asks Banas,

“Okay Where?” says Banas,

“We will be there in a few minutes!” says Banas and hangs up the phone,

Bhadra kept looking at smiling Tapi who is smiling in his dream,

“Come let's go,” says Banas downstairs,

“How about boys?” asks Netravati,

“Anyhow I will return in the morning to bring them! Don’t worry, comes let’s leave!” says Banas,

They locked the doors and left, moonlight which hit the windows and led the house to glow a blue hue. A tiring day that made Tapi sleep fast, Bhadra who is unable to understand many things from his life and slept with a lot of questions and confusion in his mind,

A bright orange light at the windows, shadow of a few birds passing together in sync, the sun turning up hotter than a day before, a red mix giant appeared as a titan in the sky, burning sense that awakes Bhadra, he removes the bedsheet and slowly comes out, with a sleepy eye turns left and right after few seconds he realized Tapi isn’t there next to him, Bhadra got down from his bed and found a table with a lot of papers and few color pencils lying all around the room he walks to the door and looks at a deep downstairs, gradually he heard a noise then got down from the stairs and found Tapi in front of the television, Bhadra crawls next to him and joins to watch television, Netravati rushed in and found both looking at the television then she walks near the television and turns off,

“Did you shower?” asks Netravati,

“We just got up mom,” says Tapi,

“Fine, get ready!” says Netravati,

Tapi gets a shower and gave some of his cloth that fit Bhadra, Bhadra wore a black shirt and the yellow trousers, Netravati walks to the bedroom with breakfast and starts to feed both, the boys chew the food so cutely which makes Netravati get tears in her eye, Tapi asks,

“Mother, why are you acting? I will eat faster don’t worry,” says Tapi,

Netravati smiles and wiped her tear and told,

“Finish it soon dear, we need to go!” says Netravati,

Netravati carrying Bhadra and holding the hands of Tapi walks faster while the titan in the sky kept up rearing that increases temperature and Netravati kept wiping the sweat, A cool night which was raged by fire is now reversed with a warm morning and a resolved blue sky, calm souls in the highway crawling with an extensive chain of people towards the town, Tapi looked at them,

“Mom who are they?” asks Tapi,

“They are tourists who were stuck in flying hills yesterday,” says Netravati,

“Okay…!” says Tapi and kept looking at everyone strangely,

“They all are returning to their houses and natives,” says Netravati,

Bhadra looked at the crowd, and all of sudden Tapi screams

“Mom… see there!!!” points toward the tourists

Netravati and also Bhadra turned,

Few the tourists were carrying the sleeping peacock in their hands and slowly marched ahead,

An intolerable pain hits Bhadra, Netravati looked at the sleeping peacock and her expression changed then she closed the eyes of both children, while Bhadra's eyes were closed but his mind kept recalling the image of the dark sleeping peacock, few seconds later Netravati takes off her hands from the children eye and starts to walk further,

“Mom, my legs are paining, I can’t walk anymore,” says Tapi,

“Tapi, keep walking, we have a long way to go dear...” says Netravati

Then she looks back expecting some vehicle for their help, but every vehicle that is passing in front of them has overloaded with the passengers, without an option they kept moving ahead,

Tired Tapi wipes his sweat and asks Mother,

“What happened to that peacock?” asks Tapi,

“Like being a seed, one fine day it breaks out of it, another day it crawls few spots of the universe to learn its existence in the paths of catastrophe, after all the struggle and obstacles, whenever it cannot fight back then it falls asleep to get a respite and passes over the legacy to its infant,

“I did not understand anything,” says Tapi,

“Don’t worry, I was trying to tell you what my father taught us” says Netravati,

“I will explain it to you later, now walk faster” murmurs Netravati and drags Tapi faster,

Bhadra on the shoulders of Netravati looks at the path behind towards the flying hills and the smoke from it hovering towards the blue sky, wondering at the endpoint of the smoke traveling to, all of a sudden Netravati drops him down, and Bhadra stood in front of many people around gazing at him, he passes the crowd and enters the house and in the middle of the hall, he found two persons sleeping with white cloth-covered their face, Netravati lifts Bhadra closer to them and Netravati told Bhadra,

“It’s the last chance for you to see your mother and father's face dear, fold your hands in front of them and pray!” says Netravati,

Bhadra looked at his mother's face, where he couldn’t see her properly a day before morning while showering him, and his dad's face which was covered with a mask all these days seemed so peaceful,

“This is your god Bhadra, please pray,” says Netravati next to his ears,

An unknown cute baby Bhadra looking at his parents sleeping without speaking to him...

He touches his mother's cheeks, suddenly a huge crying vibrancy inside the house feeling sophisticated for Bhadra to breathe, he faints down suddenly!

Netravati ran to Bhadra immediately and tried to wake him up, he slowly closes his eye with a butterfly screaming sound in his ears everything goes blank!

Fluttering sound hanging around the ears, he opened his eye slowly and saw a room full of butterflies with a shining sparkle, sun rays that strike from the broken window that communicates to a long mirror inside the room, he got down from his bed and the butterflies revolving around his legs and he carefully walks near the mirror!

A lot of butterflies around the mirror flew away, he got to see himself for the first time and kept looking at his eye deeply for a while and later rotates his eye and seemed disabled with a wing, a small wording sticker on the mirror which says,

"Only a few stars in the sky shine together and some do being apart like you and me"

Floating butterflies started to sparkle the entire room, millions of butterflies sitting on the wall flapping its wing slowly in the same sync, he looked at his neck supported by a woolen band, his heads were constantly tilting right to left, and saliva from his mouth slowly dropping down,

Tapi walks inside the room all of a sudden, the butterflies in the room disappeared rapidly and the shinning particles dropped to the ground and fade, Bhadra looks at Tapi,

"Mom told me to bring you down with all your clothes packed!" says Tapi,

"Don't worry my mother and father will take care of you from now onwards and I will be together forever, I will help you with everything like always" says Tapi,

Tapi helps Bhadra in packing meanwhile he found a drawing book of Bhadra and he opens it,

"This is the beginning of a new era!"

The second page had a painting of two birds ignited from the bottom and a massive small stones raining above it looking at each other and slowly dropping its tear,

“What an amazing paint, did you draw this?” asks Tapi,

Bhadra smiles at him shaking his head,

Tapi packs all of his cloth and carried his bag, both got down the stairs together, Bhadra slowly with disabled wings walks down to the main hall, his relatives and friends at the house were crying in front of two photos of his mom and dad, Netravati walks to him and told,

“Dear are you alright?” asks Netravati with a broken voice,

She pauses back-to-back and said,

“We have sent your parents to meet the god, we couldn’t wait for you to wake up... to be there with your parents for the Funeral,” says Netravati with an intense cry,

Unknowingly Bhadra’s eyes were dropping the shining sparkles, Netravati wiped Bhadra’s tears, Tapi and Bhadra walk closer to the photo frame and Tapi folds his hand and starts to pray, for the very first time Bhadra looks at the photo and speaks!

“I think my parents came to my height so that I can see them properly” murmurs Bhadra,

Tapi next to him opens his eye in the shock and heard him speaking,

All of a sudden, A friend of Yamuna rushed inside the house with a big scream and tear, looked at the photo, and intensely cried for a while, she looked at Netravati and asked,

"What happened to my angel," she asks,

Netravati stumbles,

"Krishna and Yamuna were intended to reach the school event, but they went to the entrance of flying hills since it was raining, later by an accident whole forest started burning, they were stuck in the middle of nowhere and caught up with the huge fire, heard of a Van driver named Atrai who struggled a lot and bought them to the hospital, but doctors couldn't help them, as they were burnt and injured very badly," says Netravati and kept crying continuously,

"My beautiful angel... Why did you leave me alone from this universe..." says Yamuna's bestie,

Bhadra inside the house looking at his parent's photo, meanwhile he heard a mysterious sound from the staircase, he looked up strangely and the sound kept increasing as he starts to climb the upstairs, there was a large terrace upon his house, the sound of a huge wings-flapping around, but he found nothing apart from Tapi stood at a corner looking at his drawing book and astonished, Bhadra walked him,

"I also do paintings, even if I am a bad painter, I do have the sense to understand the meaning at some parts of it, these sketches are relating to the scenarios of yesterday... How did you draw these situations earlier were this coincidence or did you know the future?" asks Tapi,

Bhadra looks at Tapi, shakes his head, and tried to talk but he is unable to...

"It's ok, I understand you can't speak, you can at least tilt your head from up and down if it's correct or left to right if it is wrong," says Tapi,

Bhadra with a cat-eye shakes his head and drops saliva looking at him with a smile,

"Did you draw this painting?" asks Tapi,

"Yes" speaks Bhadra,

"Oh my god, finally you spoke," says Tapi,

Tapi looks highly excited and said,

"Wait, I will bring my mother and you repeat this okay," says Tapi

And ran to bring his mother, Bhadra slowly looks around with a smile and walks to a corner looking at the flying hills,

Smoke that is still floating towards the sky, Bhadra kept staring at the tip of the flying hill transmitting smoke to a huge butterfly swag up from the bottom of the forest lifting itself towards the sky, wings of the giant that kept burning and its red reflection spread the whole town, Bhadra holds his neck and tilt up his head looking at the butterfly going near the clouds where the smoke traveled, a few seconds later, rain showers the entire village, few parts of the forest yet burning slowly turns off. Giant from the sky hovers back to the flying hills and kept rotating around the flying hills for a while with a hymn of,

I am Bhadra, son of wounded butterfly impending from the routes under a gust of catastrophic universe,
I am Yamuna, a rarest blue butterfly in the wind of families and bonds who disappeared in the sky like many in the forest,
I am Krishna, a fire butterfly surfaced in the shades of destruction, concede as the master called Art of Annihilation,

I am an invisible butterfly who initiated and traveled everybody's timeline and they call me TAPI,
I am the grey butterfly arrived in the form of soulful friendship, took Bhadra out and threw a stone upon fire woods which facilitated some calamities,
I am Hemavati, a pink butterfly ushered sayonara to the entire institution unless a sin found in Tapi's eye from one of the dark houses,
I am the old man, a water butterfly raised by the lineages to acknowledge the historical giant, chosen essence of equitable in a flow,
I am Kali, a lionhearted butterfly nearing to signify the battles to fade the menace,
I am a Giant formed alike the first letter of every chapter, every river binds together with a time that flew at a different phase of life when the survivors were in the middle of so many ups and downs emotionally, mentally, and physically yet the wings found itself a way to fly around like you and me!

ACKNOWLEDGMENTS

My sincere thanks to the readers and well-wishers from friends and family

This
Book
Was written with a lot of downs
And up in my journey of life,
However, the sculpt never
Stopped, kept going, and
Going for the progress
Of this outcome
Took me to the core of variations
Emotionally, mentally, and physically
Yet like a giant butterfly kept rotating around
The flying hills!
Wish you a
Happy
Journey

Your Butterfly is here,

www.ingramcontent.com/pod-product-compliance
Lightning Source LLC
LaVergne TN
LVHW091153150826
845672LV00005B/1131